The Season Long Awaited

ONCE UPON A DECEMBER DUOLOGY

AMBAR CORDOVA

CONTENTS

AUTHOR'S NOTE

Dear Reader,

I finished a book (The One Final Rule) back in September, and I was so happy about it. I was in love with the characters and their ending left me feeling fulfilled, which doesn't always happen. I was ready to start working on Baker Oaks five (please don't yell at me, my Baker Oaks readers who have been waiting for this book for months now) and then, an idea came to me. What if we only got a glimpse at a couple's lives once a year? What if they only saw each other once a year? But what if they also filled the in-between with one of the most beautiful, and almost lost, arts? And The Season Long Awaited came to be.

There's something magical about this story, and yes, maybe it's founded in naiveness and beliefs that might not work in the world as we know it right now, but it's filled with something I can't quite name. It's almost as if this story is as ephemeral as anything out there but also as eternal as true love.

Their story is perfect for the fans of movies like Dear John, You've Got Mail!, The Guardian, and One Day. It's perfect for the fans of love at first sight, of believing the best even when things are hard. It's perfect for those who want to believe in love again. It's perfect for you, because I truly believe if you are reading this note right now, the magic already found you. It was meant to be . . . just like Asher and Hailey's love story.

Dare I say this story is the most romantic story I've ever written. You truly can feel the love these two people have for each other oozing from the pages. You can feel their heartbeat in every line and their longing in every word—or, at the very least, I hope you do.

I also wanted to take a moment to mention I took some liberties while writing about The United States Coast Guard, specifically Aviation Survival Technicians (AST). I have the utmost respect for rescue swimmers everywhere, but this book is, in fact, fiction. If you'd like to know more about them, please visit https://www.gocoastguard.com/careers/enlisted/ast. *So Others May Live.*

Although this book started as a romantic comedy, it definitely is more like a traumatic romantic comedy, and there are some topics in this story that might be difficult for readers, and I wanted to list them for you. There's on-page explicit and consensual sex between two adults, an age gap where she's older, and profanity on page. There are mentions of child neglect, multiple sclerosis, and infertility (none of the main characters). There's an unexpected pregnancy that ends in the delivery of a healthy baby, but there's no labor on page. There are depictions of burn out, lives lost at sea, and discussions of the health care system in the United States.

I hope you love Hailey and Asher as much as I do.

143,
Ambar

PLAYLIST

Music is my love language. When I sat down to write *The Season Long Awaited,* I only had a handful of songs that described the vibes, but as soon as I finished the first draft, tens of songs started speaking to me.

Each chapter has a song (or songs) that sets the tone for that chapter. You do not have to listen to them as you read, but if you do, it will bring you into an immersive experience. If you want to listen, there's a playlist available on Spotify here, or on Apple Music here.

HAPPY LISTENING!
    Chapter 1:
    •Pretty Boy by Joji & Lil Yachty
    •Countdown by Beyoncé

CHAPTER 2:
    •Royals by Lorde
    •party 4 u by Charli xcx
    •Gooey by Glass Animals
    •Down by Marian Hill

. . .

CHAPTER 3:
- •Maine by Noah Kahan
- •Northern Attitude by Noah Kahan Ft. Hozier
- •Unwritten by Natasha Bedingfield

CHAPTER 4:
- •Breakaway by Kelly Clarkson
- •Getaway Car by Taylor Swift
- •All Of The Stars by Ed Sheeran

CHAPTER 5:
- •when the party's over by Billie Eilish

CHAPTER 6:
- •lovely by Billie Eilish & Khalid
- •PILLOWTALK by ZAYN
- •Cold War by Cautious Clay
- •Someone You Loved by Lewis Capaldi
- •Breathe Again by Sara Bareilles
- •ocean eyes by Billie Eilish

CHAPTER 7:
- •I Will Wait by Mumford & Sons
- •Collide by Howie Day

CHAPTER 8:
- •I GUESS I'M IN LOVE by Clinton Kane
- •Wildfire by Cautious Clay
- •A Thousand Years by James Arthur

. . .

CHAPTER 9:
   •Yellow by Kina Grannis

CHAPTER 10:
   •New Year's Day by Taylor Swift
   •Make You Feel My Love by Glee Cast

EPILOGUE:
   •All My Life by K-Ci & JoJo

Scan for Spotify here:

Scan for Apple Music here:

DEDICATION

To the planners and the perfectionists out there. Let yourself jump into the unknown from time to time. The most beautiful things come from the unexpected. We just can't jump ten years into the future to see how it works out. Trust the process and let go. One day, you'll find your own Asher Hunter to catch you.

And to Jayné, my own grammar perfectionist bestie. I'm so glad you offered to jump into this unexpected journey with me, unplanned and all. Everyone needs a Jayné in their life. I'm just lucky enough I have you in mine.

1

NEW YEARS EVE 2025

Pretty Boy (feat. Lil Yachty)
&
Countdown by Beyoncé

HAILEY

IT'S out of this world sweet seeing all these couples together. It's doubly sweet seeing all my friends living their best lives. It's incredibly sad I'm not at the same stage they are. Growing up, I had my list—or maybe I should say lists. My academic goals list, my accomplishments list, my relationship list. I could keep going for days. I have managed to meet every single one of them, except the one I once deemed most important of all: the relationship list. I wanted to be married with children by thirty. Instead, I'm chronically single, with barely any action since my college days, watching all my friends dance the night away in front of me at my little sister Nicole's gala.

I had Livie, my best friend, to keep me company in the singles department for a long time. That is, until last December, when she met the love of her life and is now happily married. I'm so happy for her, and maybe that's a sign my love life will be looking up soon, but I'm not holding my breath.

It's minutes away from the clock striking midnight, and here I sit by the bar, alone, again. Well, champagne keeps me company, just as it has the past few years.

"It's just you and me buddy." Talking to the champagne is new, so I guess I'll add that to my list of getting older behaviors.

I don't know what I notice first: the cold liquid running down my back or the, "Oh, I'm so sorry," from someone's lips. I slowly turn to look at a handsome guy with a now half-full cup.

"What just happened?" I ask, turning my head and trying to see how bad the damage is.

"I–I–I wasn't paying attention and I tripped. I'm so sorry." He places his glass down on the bar and grabs an obscene number of napkins to dry my back. His movements are frenetic while muttering sorry and other excuses.

"It's fine. It was an accident." But it's not fine. This dress cost an arm and a leg; I worked hard to buy it, just to have it ruined by Mr. Wasn't-Paying-Attention.

"It's not fine. It isn't. I'm sorry. Here, let's go to the bathroom real quick." He takes my hand and drags me up from the stool before I can process what's actually happening. He walks incredibly fast for someone wearing a sexy as fuck fitted tux.

And he's leading me to the bathroom . . . I can't just go to the bathroom with a complete stranger. This is how people get murdered.

"Stop!" I shout, louder than intended. He does, immediately. He lets go of my wrist and turns to face me. Concern and horror wash all over his face.

"I'm so sorry. I didn't mean to scare you. What was I thinking, dragging you like this?"

I cock my head to the side and eye him up and down. He's so good looking, oh my God. Tall, with high cheekbones and pretty dark eyes framed by slutty little glasses. The scruff around his jaw makes him look a little ragged, but the smile he's flashing me is sharp. Oh, the smile. He's smiling at me.

"What?" I ask, crossing my arms over my chest.

"You were staring."

"Oh, it must be my brain short-circuiting after having an ice cold drink spilled down my back."

He flinches. "I deserve that. May I please take you to the bathroom so we can dry your back? I would hate for a pretty dress like that to be ruined because it got wet." I'll give it to him, the man has game.

"What's your name?" I ponder the question, tasting it on my lips. Do I want to know, or am I just being difficult? My whole life, I've been called difficult, so it doesn't surprise me that's where my brain goes first.

"What?"

"If I'm stepping out of this very public place where I can scream if you try to hurt me and into a bathroom with you, I'd like to at least know your name."

"Asher." His reply is clipped, almost as if he's trying it out in his mouth. Either that's a fake name, or he's extremely shy. He might be the latter, but something tells me it might be the first.

"You don't look like an Asher." My hands land on my hips, but I hiss at the feel of the wet fabric.

"I'm sorry. Come on, let me fix it." His callused hands hold mine, and my brain goes instantly to the gutter. His hands are strong; judging by the state of them, he works with them. And I like it—a lot.

In quick strides, we step out of the ballroom, through a chandelier lit back hall, and into a family-sized bathroom with a door he locks behind him. The lights are on, triggered by movement when we step inside, and here, under them, I'm finally able to get a good look at him.

His suit is different shades of coffee, as if he mix-and-matched two to make them fit, just like I do with my bathing suits. Big ass, thick thighs, and small boobs will do that to a girl. He's wearing glasses, and while most women might not find that alluring, I do. He's giving me smart and sexy vibes.

Asher clears his throat, tilting his head to the side and giving me a once over. So I just got caught shamelessly ogling him.

Again.

Cool, cool.

"Well, are you just going to stand there, or are you going to do something about it?" I ask, and when his mahogany eyes open wide, I shake my head. "Get your head out of the gutter. That's not what I mean." So I guess this is a do-as-I-say-not-as-I-do situation now. Got it.

"Come." His voice is clipped, not apologetic like it was before. Either he was pretending back there, or he's uncomfortable now.

Which one is it, Asher? Are you sweet and kind and a little bit of a clutz, or are you an asshole who just wanted to get me into the bathroom alone?

I step forward, following his command until he leads me under the silver dryer on the wall.

"What do you expect me to do? Get on my knees under that?"

"Um, that was my plan, yes, but if that's too uncomfortable, you can always take it off." There is zero hesitation in his voice but no flirtation either. His voice is not laced with excitement and or sultriness like I would expect from a man who's trying to get into my pants.

"Wouldn't you like that?" I sass.

"Listen." He shakes his head and pinches the bridge of his nose. "If I was trying to get laid tonight, throwing a drink on a beautiful girl's dress wasn't the way to do it. So trust me when I say, I don't want to be here just as much as you don't. I'm trying, but I need you to meet me halfway."

"Woman."

"What?" he asks, stumped.

"I'm not a girl, I'm a woman. Turn around, and I'll give you the dress."

"What?"

"Am I not speaking English?" He flinches.

This—this is what people mean when they categorize me as mean. It's the way I say things, not just what I say. I thought this man was hard to read, but he's not, because that bothered him. He's either completely unfazed by this whole thing, or he's just showing me what he wants me to see.

Except that might have been triggering, because his jaw grows tight.

He lets out a sigh. "You know what? I don't need to do this. It was an accident. I was trying to help. You clearly are not happy for whatever reason, but I don't deserve for you to be condescending about it."

I obviously hurt his feelings, but what's done is done. Nothing I can do about it now, but it doesn't hurt to try to fix it. "I don't have a bra."

"At the risk of you snapping at me again, what?" he asks with effortless charm.

Oh, I'm in trouble if I'm finding this man endearing after he just asked the same question a bazillion times.

"Do you know any other question words? Or maybe how to expand on it?" I smile so he knows I'm teasing, but he doesn't react.

Damn, Hailey, you're losing your touch.

"That was a joke."

As serious as he can be, he says, "It wasn't funny."

"Yeah, I got that."

I wait for him to say something or to leave, but he doesn't do either.

"I asked you to turn around so I could take my dress off and give it to you because I'm not wearing a bra. So go ahead." I twirl my finger around in the air. He chuckles, his hand raking over his mouth and stubble, hiding a soft smile.

Okay then; we're starting to relax. That's a good sign.

He still doesn't turn, though he slowly touches the lapel of his cocoa jacket and slides it off the breadth of his shoulders. So I was right—he's definitely broader at the top than the bottom. His white shirt is carefully tucked in, showing his narrow waist and the khaki pants framing what seem like strong legs. So a gym fan, huh? Wouldn't have thought that.

"Here." He hands the jacket over, and at the raise of my eyebrow, he says, "So you can cover yourself up."

As soon as the jacket is in my hand, he turns, standing tall, his legs shoulder width apart and his arms at the front, as if he's standing at attention.

This man is an enigma, and I'm dying to figure him out, even if I just met him.

In no time, I'm out of my dress. That's what you have to do when you're single and live alone. Zippers and anything that requires another person become a nightmare. I slide his jacket on and breathe his scent in.

Damn.

He smells earthy and fresh but also like the ocean kissing my cheeks, like fire and wood after camping. It's intoxicating, the way it's invading all my senses. My lungs, my skin—it makes it all the way down to my toes.

Damn.

I walk to the dryer, and the loud woosh and warm air fill the space.

Asher turns around and shakes his head. "No, no. I'm going to do it. I messed it up."

"I can do it. I have two very capable hands. See?" I open them, spreading my fingers over the fabric.

"So what's the point of me coming in here if you were just going to do it by yourself?"

He's so damn assertive, and I like it more than I should for someone I just met. This is the longest I've been in the presence of another man who's not a patient, my dad, my brothers, or Alex, my best friend's husband, in a long time.

So maybe I'm just lonely or horny. Or both. Which would explain why I feel jittery under his gaze.

"You dragged me in here, not the other way around."

He bites his plump lower lip, closes his eyes, and lets out a breath, flaring his nostrils. "I'm not doing this. I'm sorry, it's the last time I'll say it. You're fine on your own, it seems. I will step away. Have a good night, and may 2026 bring you so much more happiness than what you have right now."

He turns to leave, and I immediately feel that loneliness creeping up again.

"Wait! Your jacket," I shout, removing it quickly. It's not until he turns around and opens his mouth to say something, the cool air hitting my nipples, that I'm reminded of my bare breasts. Too late to do anything about it now.

I extend the jacket, keeping the hand holding my dress under the dryer in place. "Here," I echo his simple offer from earlier, and he averts his gaze, almost as if my words broke *his* spell like the fire blazing in his broke mine.

He visually swallows hard, his Adam's apple bobbing and his gaze raking my body.

"It's bad manners to stare." My words shake him from his stupor, making him look at his feet. But in no time, he's holding my gaze without hesitation.

"Really? Because you've stared at me, what? Twice now?" His eyebrow lifts at the same time as he smirks, lowering his shoulders and relaxing a bit.

I like it. A lot.

Asher starts walking toward me in long but shaky strides until he's standing in front of me, tall, broad, and absolutely delicious. I search his face for a sign he feels this chemistry between us, that he feels maybe an ounce of this electricity, but my efforts are futile, because he gives me nothing. Relaxed? Yes, but that's it.

The loud whooshing of the dryer and my erratic heartbeat take over my ears, but nothing else. Not a sound, not a word, not even a look from Asher my way. I should probably step back or cover myself, but I'm too shaken to do so. No, not shaken—awestruck by this mysterious man.

Who are you, Asher, and what's going on inside that head?

It's like he can hear my thoughts, because his eyes finally snap back to me, and with a tight jaw, he stretches his hand forward, over me, and pulls one, two, three paper towels in rapid succession. I blink, and he's wetting them. I have no time to question him, because in one, quick move, he's standing behind me.

He parts my hair and smooths it over my shoulders. As my breath catches, he whispers, "Wet."

He clears his throat. "This is wet, sorry."

It's not only wet, but it's cold, and I twitch as he wipes my back tenderly, a complete juxtaposition to his behavior. He's fumbling with words, yet his touch is steady. He won't look at me when I'm standing practically naked in front of him, but he swallowed so hard, I thought he would break his throat.

Are your puzzle pieces all jumbled up, Asher? Can I play too? Can I put them together?

Loud cheers in the distance startle me, and apparently him too, since the soft and delicate touches on my back disappear. I pat my dress again to find it warm and dry. I check my watch—almost midnight, but not quite yet. Maybe a minute to go.

I slide the red dress over my head, tugging gently down. Something stronger pulls with me, and when I look back, I realize Asher is helping.

"Thanks." I offer him a smile, one he mirrors.

"Sorry. This is not how I envisioned spending New Year's Eve, and it threw me off." He lets out a breath that seems to have come from deep within, like he'd been holding it.

"I don't think this is how I imagined it either," I reply, although if I'm honest with myself, being locked away with a handsome man so terrified of doing the wrong thing, he won't even look at me isn't so bad. He seems to be a gentleman, and it's been a while since I've been around one of those.

"How exactly did you picture it?" I ask, partly because it's the polite thing to do but also because I'm intrigued.

"A champagne flute in hand and my lips on a pretty girl's mouth by the time the clock struck midnight." The answer surprises us both, and while I chuckle, his eyes grow wider by the second. "Sorry," he mutters.

"Why? You were honest." I look down at my watch again. It's not midnight yet, but the cheers are getting louder outside. We're close. So close.

I grab his hand and attempt to pull him out, but he won't budge. "Come on. We still have time to make that happen. If you consider me pretty, that is." I wink his way, and he lets me pull him out of the bathroom into the main ballroom.

Servers walk around with champagne flutes balanced on trays, and I approach one quickly, Asher's hand in mine as I take a glass.

"For you." I hand him the flute before grabbing one of my own and smiling faintly at the server.

"Twenty!" The countdown begins as the crowd shouts in unison, watching the shrimp drop. Such a weird thing to do, but this town is weird like that.

Asher looks spooked, and it just hits me—he might have been here with someone.

Oh, Hailey, you clueless girl. That's why he's been so on edge and giving you mixed signals. You made him uncomfortable.

"Fifteen!" The countdown continues. I'm about to put this man out of his misery.

"Why don't you just go find whoever you came here with? I was wrong to assume you were here alone and needed to find someone to kiss at midnight." The apology tastes bitter on my lips, naturally—my body isn't used to them.

"What?" he asks, making me laugh. He loves that word, doesn't he?

"Ten!" Louder this time.

"Go. You're going to miss the midnight kiss with whoever you came here with. Go! Go!"

I press my hand behind his back to usher him away, but he's like solid stone. No, more like an oak tree. Tall, broad, and strong.

"Six!"

"Is that what you think? That I somehow came here with a girl and I, what? Ditched her so I could dry your back?"

Well, that sounds silly now that he says it like that, doesn't it?

"Five!"

He takes a step forward, in the opposite direction of where I thought he would go. He's standing so close to me, but I still have to tilt my head back to peer up at him through my eyelashes.

"It's not," he whispers, bringing his hand to cup my face.

"Three!"

He searches my eyes. "I didn't, and if you let me, I would love for you to be my midnight and birthday kiss."

"Wait, it's your birthday?"

"Two!"

"Yes or no?" he asks, my heart racing with the imaginary tick of the clock.

"One!"

"Yes," I whisper in a rush, and with the loud cheers from the shrimp dropping and the clock striking midnight, he crashes his mouth to mine.

His lips are the opposite of him. It seems like he's just a giant, walking contradiction. Where his stride and his actions were hesitant and almost unsure, his kiss is anything but. He kisses me softly yet possessively. His plump lips explore mine as his fingers rake through my hair to the back of my head, leaving goosebumps behind.

Something cold and wet touches my back, and if I'm guessing correctly it's his champagne flute as he pulls me closer to him. His tongue strokes my bottom lip gently, asking for permission, and I grant him access. My hands, limp at my side, are itching to touch, to grab, to feel, so I stop overthinking and just do it. If his tongue is deep in my mouth, I sure as hell can touch him.

I slide my hand up his back, keeping the one holding the champagne to the side, but he flinches at the touch. I stop. I stop my hand from moving, my lips from exploring, and break the spell. The world around us didn't stop like I thought it did. The music is playing louder than it was before, and people are dancing, celebrating the new year.

"Sorry," I whisper against his lips. Another apology. Who am I today?

"I'm not."

"For touching you, I mean. I didn't ask permission, and it made you uncomfortable."

He shakes his head. "It didn't. I just wasn't expecting it. I . . . " He scratches his head. "I got lost for a second."

His breath tickles my lips, all sweet and smokey, just like him. It's intoxicating, dizzying, and just . . . wow.

"Did you say it was your birthday?" I change the topic; I can't keep thinking about how this kiss might have changed my life, because I sound like a naive girl from a classic cliche romance movie. He doesn't answer, though; he just nods.

"Well, happy New Year and happy birthday, Asher. I hope that kiss was exactly what you envisioned for the New Year." I wink, bringing flirty Hailey back.

"There you are! Happy New Year, babe!" Livie shouts, wrapping her arms around me. I turn to hug my best friend and breathe out for the first time in the past, what? Twenty minutes? It has only been that short amount of time since he spilled that drink on me?

Twenty minutes, and I'm wondering what else I get to do with this man. If that doesn't say new year, new me, I don't know what does.

I break the warmest hug and smile at her. "Happy New Year!"

"Where were you? We were looking all over," Livie adds.

"Happy New Year, Hailey," her husband, Alex, says.

"Sorry, I got a little distracted." I smile at my friends shyly, surely blushing.

"Alex, Livie this is—" The words die in my mouth when I don't see Asher anymore. It's like he disappeared.

Poof, gone.

I look around, but all I see are streamers, lights, glasses clinking in the air, and the celebration happening everywhere. There's not one sight of this man.

"What?" Livie asks, clearly confused.

"Did you—"

"Happy New Year, sis!" Nicole interrupts, wrapping me up in a hug too. That opens the door to an abundance of celebratory hugs and cheers—one after the other, siblings, friends, and Nicole's coworkers.

I'm hugged out by the end, but I don't stop searching. It's futile, though, because I don't see him again. As time passes, I start to wonder if I made it all up.

Am I *that* lonely that I conjured a person into existence?

2

NEW YEARS EVE 2026

Royals by Lorde • Party 4 u by Charli xcx • Gooey by Glass Animals

ASHER

"OUT OF ALL THE places in the world, Amelia Island is where you want to spend your first long leave?" Travis asks. "This place doesn't exactly scream party hard and forget it all for two days."

"You didn't have to come." I step through the doors of the ballroom to find it exactly the same as last year: decorated to the nines, loud with chatter, and filled with people dancing and celebrating. Crashing this gala last year was a blessing and a curse, but this year, I bought a ticket like everyone else, so I won't be shying away from enjoying my time and seeing if I can find *her*.

"And what? I don't even have anywhere to call home anymore. You're stuck with me, buddy."

I shake my head, leading the way through the crowd of designer dresses and strong perfume. But none smell like oranges. None smell like delicate fresh citrus. None have perfect breasts behind a red dress or a quiet but pretty smile she hides away. None of them have long, dark hair mimicking my soul, or cute bangs kissing her eyebrows as if they're meant to coexist. None of these women are her.

Her, because I didn't even get her name.

Her, because I left before I could ask anything.

Her, because I haven't stopped thinking about that kiss and the angel who carried those lips.

"Two beers, please," Travis tells the bartender, who doesn't ID us. Just like last year. Except this year, I'm actually legal to drink. Technically, I was last year too—at least I was when I downed the champagne glass when I was already drunk. Drunk on her kiss and her scent. Drunk on the feel of her soft, delicate skin under my rough hands. Drunk on her.

"Wait a damn minute. Are you here because of your mystery girl? I thought you wanted to come back now we could actually afford a ticket and do it right . . . but you're hoping she's here, aren't you?" he asks.

I bring the glass to my lips and take a sip of the worst-poured beer I've ever tasted. I don't understand why they must pour it into a glass instead of just keeping it in the vessel it arrives in, all in the name of etiquette. It's a waste of time and good beer.

My eyes search silently, ignoring Travis' question. I know the chances are slim, but this is my last attempt. I haven't been able to find her, not in pictures tagged from last year on social media or in the thousands of profiles with Amelia Island listed as her place of residence I found online. Nobody here looks like her either.

"Fine. If you won't answer my question, I'm gonna go enjoy my time." He gets up, grabs his glass, and pats my back. "For what it's worth, I don't think she's real, man. Nobody gets so stuck into someone's brain to the point they can't stop thinking about them for a whole year after one kiss."

He walks away, leaving me with the same thoughts I've had for a year. I know I didn't make her up. I know she exists. I know it deep in my bones. I just hope I can find out who she is.

The room is buzzing with energy, and when Lorde's *Royals* blasts through the speaker followed by loud cheers, a multitude of people rush to the dance floor.

Right there, at the edge of the dance floor, there's a very loud and lively girl shouting the song at the top of her lungs. My heart skips a beat and my breath catches in my throat. Dancing across from her, in a royal blue dress with dark lipstick and beads of sweat sliding down her neck, it's *her*.

She dances to the song in the opposite way of her friend. Her friend, or who I assume is her friend, bounces on the balls of her feet, the giant, puffy skirt of her dress bunched in her hands as she shouts the lyrics. My mystery girl just sways side to side and sips on a dark liquid I assume is wine. Her bangs are slightly stuck to her forehead and, judging by the sweat kissing her body, she's been dancing for a while.

I will her to look at me, but she's entirely lost in this song. The chorus hits again, and with it, her hands fly up as her body rolls to the beat. Her body is like an illusion, and mine is having the hardest time doing anything other than keeping my eyes on her. The beat drops, and loud cheers erupt. I use that as my cue. Even if I have to tell my body to follow suit and my dick to calm the fuck down, I decide to walk up to her and see if she remembers me. She has to.

What we experienced last year couldn't just be in my head. I know she felt it too. But where I was lost in mine and practicing self-control not to fuck her mouth in that bathroom so she could stop over-thinking, she was as forward as possible. At least, forward with her questions. I wish she would have just given me a sign she wanted me to do something, but we were in a tough position, one she didn't show she wanted to be a part of before I led her to the bathroom. I couldn't also make the first move.

I didn't want her to feel pressured into doing anything . . . but then, she kissed me.

My life has been suspended in this worm hole of possibilities ever since.

Three hundred sixty five days, I've been thinking about this girl.

Three hundred sixty five days, I've been stroking my dick to the sight of her in high heels and a tiny thong, those perky breasts she flashed me accidentally.

A whole year of dreaming of this girl, and she's finally here.

Woman. She's a woman. Her words from a year ago echo in my head as I reach her on the dance floor.

Her eyes stay closed, even when my hand snakes across her belly, pulling her body flush against mine. She tilts her head back, and dark, thick eyelashes kiss her cheeks as she whispers the lyrics. Her friend's puzzled look vanishes when another man does the same as me, and dances with her. She jumps up and down in his arms and dances away, but my attention is back on my mystery girl.

My mystery girl who grinds her perfect ass against my dick. So much for me keeping it calm. There's no way I'll be able to now. I slide my hands to her hips, holding them in place as I whisper in her ear. "I'm so glad to know you weren't a figment of my imagination."

She tenses, stopping all movement and snapping her eyes open at the same time the song transitions.

"Asher," she whispers, turning in my arms and searching my eyes. What for? Not sure, but she's not stepping back, which is a big deal . . . and she remembers my name.

"Mystery girl." My smile widens at her reaction. Soft smile, pretty, glimmering eyes, and flushed, rosy cheeks. Just like I remember, except better somehow.

"Mystery girl, huh?" she asks, not moving one bit now. My fingers dig deeper into her hips, willing her to move, and she takes the unspoken cue. Even though the thunderous beat vibrates through the speaker, my eyes and ears are laser focused on her.

"What else was I supposed to call you? You never told me your name."

"I didn't think you were real," she whispers, and I open my arms, showing her my body.

"I am. In the flesh."

She cocks her head to the side. "Permission to touch?"

As if she couldn't be any more perfect already, asking for permission does it. I nod, allowing her to do as she wants. Her hands graze my chest tentatively, as if I'm a ticking bomb she's trying to defuse.

She's more on point than she thinks, proceeding with caution, but damn it if I don't want to be reckless and allow her to touch as much as she wants.

Her fingers continue to my neck and my tense jaw. I didn't know I was clenching it until she caresses my jawline gently.

"You shaved," she whispers, not stopping her fingers as they ghost over my phantom mustache delicately. Her fingertips feel like soft feathers over my skin, and it's too much.

Too much.

My hands grip hers, changing their trajectory and placing them on my shoulders instead.

"I did." I didn't tell her anything particular about me, just my name, and I want it to stay that way. Nobody calls me Asher, so it makes it even more special, as if it was just me and her in this moment, a reality where only we exist.

"Where did your glasses go?" she asks, tracing my eyebrows.

"Contacts." I'm lost in her eyes, in the deep gray of them. They look like the ocean, salt kissed, impossible to forget. "You still haven't told me your name, beautiful."

"Did your voice change? It's deeper now."

She might be deflecting, but she's not wrong. It does sound deeper. Twenty, too young to drink but old enough to go to war. Twenty, too young to rent a car but old enough to parent a child or carry a gun. This is backwards as fuck and always has been.

"You just remember it wrong," I reply, turning her body and drawing her back flush against me. I'm afraid she'll see right through me if I don't put some sort of distance between us, but I don't want there to be any. I just need a second to compose myself and not give her the shy kid she got last time.

She drags her nails up my thighs, leaving pure fire behind, even if there's zero contact with my skin. We both shiver when her ass grinds back against my hard dick. Her skin breaks into goosebumps under my touch, and the air leaves my lungs as if I was underwater and I need air. I need her.

"Have you been thinking about me too, mystery girl?" I whisper against the shell of her ear. I can feel the smile on her face even if I can't see it, and almost as if she was psychic, she tilts her head back and shows me. The most wicked smile I've ever seen steals the oxygen from my lungs—and my dick—once more.

"Why don't we get out of here and I'll show you how much?" Shit. I lace my fingers with hers, and she starts walking right back to where we were a year ago. Back to the giant bathroom tucked in the hallway.

She opens the door before I can offer to do it for her and steps to the side to allow me in. She's not looking at anything but what's in front of her, so I guess she's not even a little bit worried people might know why we're both in the bathroom. The door shuts tight behind her, and she rises up on her tiptoes to kiss me. She doesn't touch me with anything but her lips, but fuck that. I want to touch. I want to touch everything.

I want to see if her nipples are as hard as I thought they were last time. I want to trace her slim back all the way to the curve of her ass barely hidden by that lace fabric. I want to inhale her whole and make her mine, even if I don't know her name.

Sweet, soft lips taste faintly of grapes and lust as they kiss me, and it's better than I remember. My hands roam her back, pulling her closer as I walk us back toward the bathroom door. I turn the latch, making sure it's locked before I gently push her body against the door. She gasps into my lips.

"You have no clue how often I've thought about your lips on mine again. About your citrusy scent invading my senses again."

"Is this what was hiding underneath the shy boy persona? This possessive man who tells me his thoughts and doesn't simplify every-thing to a one word question?" she sasses.

I turn her around, pinning her arms above her head with one hand and tracing the round ass in front of me with the other. "This posses-sive man will spank this perfect ass if you keep sassing me like that." My voice is rough against her neck.

"That's exactly what I wanted to do last year, but I had to control myself. How do we feel about that? Huh?" I kiss her gently.

"How I feel about what?" she murmurs, her voice doing more to me than my wildest dreams. "Sassing you, or you spanking my ass for being mouthy?"

I groan. "Both."

"Try it and find out." She pushes her ass against my hand harshly, and I see stars. I will die in this bathroom with this girl grinding on me, happy this is how I go.

"You're going to be the death of me," I mutter.

"Tick, tock, Asher. Are you a man of your word, or are—"

I spank her, right in the middle of her ass cheek, earning me a hot as sin whimper.

We like it.

Got it.

"You were saying?" she asks, but her voice shifts from sassy to lustful.

"Where is it okay for me to touch?" I grab her ass gently, and she spreads her legs.

"Everywhere. Please."

"So, so polite." I raise her dress up her legs and over her ass. A black lace thong barely covers anything, and I groan.

"Hands on the door, yeah?" She nods at my suggestion.

I slide her underwear down, and she promptly steps out of them. I use this as my cue to sit under her, back against the wall, her perfect pussy right in front of me. She looks down, keeping her hands on the door, just like I told her to.

"Can I kiss everywhere too?" I ask, smiling at her.

"Fuck, yes. Please," she begs, sticky lust guiding her words.

My hands find her ass, quickly pulling her to me, and in one, quick swoop, my tongue slides through her folds.

"Fuck," she whispers as I groan against her slick sex. She not only smells like oranges, she tastes citrusy too. Or tropical, maybe. Pineapple and lemon, mixed with whatever other perfect taste. How does this girl look like that, smell and taste like this, and she's walking around without a ring on her finger?

I take my time licking and teasing every inch of this gift. She lifts a knee, letting it rest on my shoulder and bucking against my face. The taste of her arousal changes, and fuck, if I don't like it even more. I lick, lap, and suck at everything, flicking my tongue over her clit and grabbing her ass harder.

"Yes," she whispers, all breathy and spent.

I won't stop. I want her orgasm almost as relentlessly as I want her name. If this was another time, maybe another lifetime, I would want more from her, but claiming her orgasm is enough for me, at least for now. Her legs quiver around me, and I suck her clit into my mouth, hard. She explodes.

She swirls her hips, barely able to move as she grinds closer and tighter to my face. As if she could come any closer. As if she could come any harder.

"Fuck!" she shouts as I groan, and with quick, shuddering breaths, she relaxes, and I let go.

"You taste perfect."

"Thanks," she whispers, and we both laugh. I slide myself up between her and the wooden door pressing hard against my back. She doesn't waste any time, and her lips are back on mine. Her hand lowers to grab my dick, and now I'm the one moaning.

"Do you think you can fuck me right now?" she asks.

"Baby, I would give you anything you want right now, but I don't have a condom on me. I didn't think I would find you today, let alone have sex with you. I'm good, I promise." I kiss her lips, just long enough to leave me wanting more but short enough that my dick won't get any more ideas.

"Promise you won't kill me," she says with a smile on her face.

"Scout's honor." I kiss my index and middle fingers and lift them in the air.

She unlocks the door. "Pick those up and let's go." She opens the door and steps through, leading the way who knows where, but I grab her thong and gladly follow.

♫ DOWN *by Marian Hill*

. . .

THE SEASON LONG AWAITED 29

"AT THE RISK of sounding like a stalker, is this where you live?" I ask as we walk through the front door of what seems like a Victorian hotel.

She chuckles, turning back with a smile on her face that stops me in my tracks. "No, I wouldn't be bringing a stranger into my house the second time I meet him . . . and I'm not local. This is a hotel."

The reception area is dark and quiet, the probability of someone working right now slim. This is reckless; if I was a dangerous man, she'd have no way of alerting anyone else.

"I'm not a stranger. You are." My whispers carry through the space as we continue down a corridor and stop in front of a room. A room she opens with a key from the case on her phone. The entire room smells like her: oranges, lemons, maybe even grapefruit, like a citrus fruit salad exploded.

"I'm as much of a stranger to you as you are to me," she replies, turning and letting her dress drop to her feet, leaving her in those sexy as hell heels and nothing else.

"I still don't know your name."

My strides reach her quickly, careful not to touch, as if she's made of glass and I might break her. I want her to say she wants me before I go any further. Her body does, but I want words. I want to hear her say it, and I want her to tell me her damn name.

"Top drawer." Half the time, she makes zero sense. Top drawer what?

"What?" That makes her smile wider, and I roll my eyes. She points to a drawer, where I find a clear bag full of condoms. "Came prepared, huh?"

"I'm always prepared, and I'll tell you what." She bites the corner of her lower lip, right where I want to bite myself. "Make me come again, and I'll tell you my name. But hurry, because I told my friends if they don't hear from me in the next hour, send the police."

She twirls her hair in her hand and tosses it over her shoulder, allowing her breasts to be on full display. My dick sure as hell is happy to see them. She says we don't have time; I can work with that. I've been ready to be inside her for a whole ass year.

"How do you like to be fucked, mystery girl?" I step out of my shoes and closer to her.

"Slow and tender." Her skin breaks out in goosebumps under my careful touch down her arm.

"Fast and deep." The space between us is practically non-existent now, and she catches a breath.

I lower my lips to the shell of her ear, breathing her all the way in and whispering, "Or you don't care, just as long as I have you screaming my name."

She shudders. "I'm not a screamer."

"I would love to test that theory." I cup her face with one hand, allowing me to hold her in place while I lick her neck—oh, she tastes so sweet.

She tilts her head back, granting me better access, and I bite tenderly. She hisses and arches her back, pressing her chest to mine.

"Go ahead. See what you find out," she sasses.

Fuck yes.

"I've been thinking about this moment for a year." I hold her face in my hands and stare at her, hoping my gaze reaches her soul. Have I invaded all her fantasies and dreams as she has mine?

"Get on your knees on the bed."

She blushes and nods, walking backwards, her heated gaze eating me alive as I take my clothes off. "Is that a thigh tattoo?"

I nod, bringing my index finger to my lips. "Shh, it's a secret." This little tattoo almost got me in trouble with my parents, who are 'your body is your temple' fanatics and didn't allow tattoos. The first thing I said I was going to do after leaving their house was get tattoos every-where, but I haven't had time at all. So just one, a small rock with waves crashing on it. My little rebellious act.

She reaches down to take her shoes off, but I shake my head, stop-ping her from doing it. "Those stay on."

Her gray eyes linger on my body, raking every part of me. When they reach mine, I smirk. "So tell me—what's better: your dreams or reality?"

"Funny, I don't seem to remember telling you I've been dreaming of you." She's so sassy, and all I want to do is fuck that mouth of hers and see what she thinks of that.

"We both know you did . . . but let me answer that for you." I reach for her, my hands digging into her hips and flipping her over, pushing gently until her hands touch the bed. "I'm about to give you something to dream about." She eyes me sheepishly, and I smile. "Get on the bed."

She climbs up, her perfect ass practically in my face, testing me, teasing me. My handprint is still on her right cheek. I lick the mark and then kiss it, whispering into her flesh, "I'm sorry for this."

"I'm not." She pushes her ass back, pressing against my lips. I smile; what else can I do?

"Anything off limits?" I ask.

"I'll tell you if I don't like something." Could she be more perfect? I slide my tongue down the curve of her ass and onto her thigh, using my hands to spread her open, giving me the view I've been dreaming of. Fuck, she's so wet, her pussy glistening and her puckered hole begging to be touched. I don't think I considered myself an ass man until her, but damn, if I don't want to lick and eat it whole. Lick and eat *her* whole.

I swipe my tongue over it, and she squeezes on a flinch but then relaxes against my tongue.

"Yes," she moans. *Yes*, indeed. I lick and tease her, feeling it all the way down to my toes. Her pleasure is intertwined with mine at this point, as if I've known her for longer. As if my body decided that the year of torture I put us through thinking about her is enough for my brain to believe she's essential to my pleasure. Her arousal drips onto my fingers as I touch and explore, getting her ready for me. She bucks her ass against my face when I slide two fingers into her pussy, arching her back and asking for more.

"I have exactly what you need." On my knees, I slide the condom on, and in one, quick thrust, I bury myself inside her. I groan, she moans, and the wave of pleasure rolling through my body is enough for me to know I will make a fool of myself and not last long.

I press her back down, her forearms giving out and her face resting on the mattress. The angle allows me to touch the spot I know will drive her over the edge, and she seems to know it too, judging by the pillow she's biting. I reach forward, sliding in deeper and pull the pillow away from her face. "I want to hear you when you do, *indeed*, scream my name."

The sound from her lips is more like a whimper. If I can help it, I will make her come so hard, she won't have any choice but to say my name. She won't have any choice but to lose control. I'm not taking a no for an answer.

I slam into her, digging my fingertips into her hips, harder and deeper with every thrust. She's so wet, it coats both our legs and makes indecent sounds. In between moans, groans, and slapping noises, her pussy clenches around my dick. She's close—I can feel it.

"Touch yourself," I command, and she follows immediately, feeding my ego and my need to have this moment be exactly what I hoped.

"Ash," she whispers, all breathy and spent, and fuck, just the sound alone could make me come.

"Come on, baby. Give it to me." In and out, fast, hard, deep. In and out, long thrusts and her perfect little moans. I hold her hair in my hand, gently wrapping it around my fist, allowing her time to protest if she doesn't like it. She arches back more, not moving her head from the mattress but clenching her thighs. Yes, ma'am. Let's go.

I bend forward, pulling her soft, dark hair, driving deeper, digging my fingertips into her skin, feeling her shake under my touch.

"Ash!" she screams, and with it, I come too. Her tight pussy squeezing me, the nickname she gave me that only she uses dancing in my brain, and the wave of mutual pleasure taking me to the deepest end . . .

My groan fills the space, guttural, deep, raw, until we're both limp and spent, but I can't slip out. Not yet. What if this is a dream? What if this is only in my imagination, and the minute I stop touching her, she disappears?

My forehead rests on her back as I let go of her hair and kiss her gently. I do what I have to and slide out of this girl, walking to the bathroom to toss the used condom, clean up, and rinse my face. Focus, Hunter, Focus. I walk back to her, towel wrapped around my waist, but what I see is not what I pictured. I thought she would be in bed still, waiting for me. I didn't take long in the bathroom, after all. Instead, I catch the last the last glimpse of her body before the dress dances over her skin as she slides it all the way down.

"What are you doing?" I ask, praying it's not what I think it is. She's, what? Done? She's leaving? What's happening?

"I have to go back. My little sister is in charge of the gala, and I need to be there for the shrimp drop. You can come back with me, or you can stay. Up to you."

She fixes her bangs in the mirror, reapplies her lipstick, and grabs her purse like we just didn't have the best sex of my life.

"Just like that?" I ask.

"What do you expect me to do, Asher? Stay here and share my life with you? This was fun. We got it out of our systems, and now we can move on. I'm sure all the pent up angst from not fucking each other last year is what drove us to this, but now, it's over."

She opens the door but stops, turning around and looking me up and down, as if she just realized I'm still standing naked in my blue fuzzy socks, my clothes on the ground.

"You fucked me with socks on?" she asks, suppressing a laugh.

"I had no time to take them off. Someone's needy pussy was waiting for my dick." I hold my hips, not hiding, letting her see as much as she wants to see.

"Let me get dressed and I'll go back with you, yeah?" She nods, stepping out and pulling the door with her.

Except she doesn't close it all the way. She slides her head in and says, "It's Hailey, by the way."

"What?" I ask, knowing damn well it will make her smile, and it does.

She scoffs, shaking her head, a giant smile on her face. "My name. My name is Hailey." She closes the door behind her, leaving me here, rattled. It's not normal to feel like this about someone after only seeing them twice, right?

"So last year, you said it was your birthday," Hailey says from the driver's seat on the way to the venue. The drive is short, so we don't actually have a lot of time to talk, but considering we practically know nothing about each other, it's good we get some sort of time to chat. Not that anything serious can come out of this, considering I go to A School in a couple of weeks.

Training to be a rescue swimmer has been a dream of mine since I can remember, and I've worked hard to make it a reality. Despite my parents thinking I'm a waste of time and space, this is what I'm meant to do. It's a shame Hailey doesn't fit into those plans, because it could've been fun.

"Tomorrow is my birthday."

"New Year's Day baby, huh?" The vent blasts cool air into the car and makes Hailey's bangs dance in her face. *Oh yeah, my birthday is tomorrow, and my wish is to see you again.* I can't say that without sounding needy as fuck, though.

"Mmm-hmm." It's all I say when the reality is, apparently, I was born to ruin my parents' years until the end of time. "Son, you came on the first day of the year to remind us of the new life you brought, one of never-ending bills and working until dusk.' If I had a penny for every time my father reminded me of how much of an inconvenience I was, I would be rich by now.

"Did my pussy eat your words?" I choke on my spit at her words.

"What?"

"Here we go again. What happened to the commanding and talkative Asher, huh? Now we're back to monosyllables." What do I say? I'm being careful not to share too much? Because something about you makes me want to put my guard down? Do I tell her I'm afraid if I open my mouth to say anything, the only thing that will come out is how badly I want to see her again but I can't? I can't. My job. The distance. Everything.

"I'm a private person, Hailey. But I do like sex." She looks my way, raising an eyebrow. "I liked sex with you."

She shakes her head, leading us to the valet and stepping out before either of us can open the door for her. She does the same with the glass door framing the entrance to the gala venue. I speed up to catch up with her, but I can't, because Travis rushes over the minute he sees me.

"Where were you? We have to go." He doesn't say anything else, but his urgency is clear. Something happened; there's no doubt about it.

"What? Where?" I ask. Hailey is watching attentively.

"I'll explain in the car, but something happened with Holt. We have to go back." I shake my head.

"Okay. Got it." I look back at Hailey, mouthing a sorry. "Give me two minutes."

Travis looks at Hailey and smiles before tipping an invisible hat and saluting her. "Two minutes."

Travis walks away, leaving just the two of us standing under a chandelier.

"I guess this is our fate: seeing each other for a few hours on New Year's Eve while you disappear like Cinderella as the clock strikes midnight," Hailey adds, pointing at the clock on the wall showing there's only a minute to midnight.

"I guess so." She closes the space between us, holding my face and staring right into my soul.

"I'm not in a position to do anything with anyone for more than what tonight was," she whispers, smiling at me. Good, because neither can I. I just nod. "But let's say if you find yourself on Amelia Island again next New Year's Eve, you know where to find me."

The cheers in the distance announce the countdown.

"And what? You'll be waiting for me?" I ask, and she nods.

"If the stars align and the seasons change, I will wait for our next moment right here. I promise to give you more than a few hours next time."

I cock my head to the side and consider her. It seems too good to be true. I don't have to share with her why this is the best case scenario for me.

"What are the parameters?" I ask so at least we're both on the same page.

"None. Don't complicate this. If you find someone to love between now and then, just don't come back. I'll do the same. If not . . . see you in a year."

I kiss her lips gently as the crowd erupts into cheers in the distance. "Happy New Year, Hailey. See you next December."

Our foreheads touch as she whispers against my lips, "Happy Birthday, Ash. See you next December." She steps back, leaving me empty handed as she sways her hips back to the party.

"See you in twelve months!" she shouts, and I feel her absence even more. I'm destined to miss this girl I barely know forever, but I have no time to question anything. I have no other choice.

I run outside to Travis' car, where he tells me Holt, one of our friends, was in an accident in North Carolina, where he was waiting for us to start training. As we drive all night to get to him, I think about how, at the very least, for the first time in my life, I have something to look forward to this year. Happy birthday to me.

JUNE, 2027

Dear Hailey,

At the risk of sounding like a stalker I think, I found you. It wasn't an easy feat, let me say, but after you mentioned your little sister ran the gala, it helped me narrow it down. I hope this is actually you and not a random person I found on the internet. You don't live on Amelia Island, do you? Maybe that's why I couldn't find you the first time. If this isn't you, I would stop reading right now, because this is about to get awkward as shit.

Pardon me for not writing to you for six months, but I was going through training hell and needed to stay focused. We didn't talk much about what we do for a living, and I don't know if you're willing to share, but you'll see my return address is a Coast Guard station. That's accurate, and I can say that this year, at twenty-two, my dream came true. You're looking, or reading, I guess, at a Class of 2026 graduate of the A School, Aviation Survival Technician— a rescue swimmer, in layman's terms. This is another reason why our arrangement worked for me. I also am not in the position to be in a relationship with anyone. I did request leave for New Year's Eve; my new station granted it, so I will be there this December. I already got my ticket and everything. I know you said your sister organizes the gala, but if you're willing to go as my date, I'm attaching a confirmation for your ticket too. Either way, it'll be okay, whether you show up or I'm there on my own. All the money goes to a good cause, right?

I hope this letter finds you well, and that if you're still single on December 31st, you meet me at our spot.

With kindness,

Ash

NOVEMBER, 2027

Dear Asher,

Or should I say Hunt, since now that I know your full name, I was also able to find you. Huntswimsforyou? Cute as fuck handle. Why did you let me call you Asher if everyone calls you Hunt? Or Hunter? Was I not worthy of knowing your last name?

I appreciate you finding me, and maybe it was a little stalker-ish, but nothing a public search wouldn't give you. Congratulations on graduating! That sounds amazing. I know nothing about rescue swimmers, but I will read my heart out about it so we can chat in December.

Yes, I'm still single, and yes, I'll be your date. I doubt I'll get a boyfriend in the next month or so, considering I'm writing this in November. Truth is, your letter caught me off guard, and I slid it into my bag. I forgot about it until it was time to clean it out. Not that I forgot you, but there's just been a lot going on.

I also work saving lives. Not like you, but with children. It's been a tough year as a peds trauma nurse, and it's been even harder to balance it all. I actually don't know why I'm sharing all of this, but maybe you'd understand, since you have a servant heart too.

Also . . . you're only twenty-two? You should've said some-

thing! I'm almost ten years older than you. Does that make me a cougar? I'm a cougar now, aren't I?

Can I tell you a secret? I've been looking forward to this gala all year. I hope I do get to see you in a month or so.

Stay safe out there.

Xo,

Hales

3

NEW YEARS EVE 2027

Maine by Noah Kahan • Northern Attitude by Noah Kahan Feat. Hozier • Unwritten by Natasha Bedingfield

HAILEY

WHY AM I SO NERVOUS? It's not like this man hasn't seen everything and licked it too, or like there's anything on the line other than a good time. We've been clear. Neither of us is in a position to have a relationship with anyone. Do I want a relationship? Yes, but my life has gone to shit this year, and adding anything to my never-ending list of things to do just doesn't seem possible.

He offered to pick me up, and because he already knew where I was staying in Amelia, I said yes. He's picking me up early enough to be my date to the dinner portion of the event, and I'm nervous as fuck. I'm wearing the red dress I wore the year I met him. If he remembers, he'll see how special I think it is that our paths are crossing again, how special I think this whole thing is. The electric feeling coursing through my veins is something I haven't felt in years, not since I had a crush on Timmy Mcfair in ninth grade, actually.

The quiet knock on the door startles me. He's early. *Hot.* Nothing I love more than punctuality.

Okay, Hailey. It's show time.

The sight waiting for me on the other side of the door steals my breath away. There, as handsome as ever, is Asher—or Hunt, I should say—in the same khaki suit combo he had on two years ago, his mustache back on his face alongside his slutty little glasses. It's almost as if we were suspended in time two years ago. I'd love to imagine that's the reality, considering the wrinkles around my eyes and my never-ending backache reminding me I'm not in my twenties anymore.

My mother always acted like she was breaking when my siblings were little. I thought it was a defense mechanism to get me to pick up and do more chores, since I'm ten years older, but now that I'm in my thirties, I get it. Shit's hard, and we're all just trying our best.

"Well hello there, Hunt." Ugh, I hate how that name rolls off my lips. He seems to think the same, because he looks like he's gonna throw up.

"Don't call me that."

"Well, that's what most people call you, no?" I stay in front of the door as if I have no manners, but somehow, my feet are superglued to the ground, and he's a fast drying fan blowing straight my way.

"But you're not most people."

He doesn't finish his sentence, and I don't know if it's the distance or the time, but does he look even more handsome now? It's unbelievable how much someone can change in two years. Like rougher or edgier? Or am I just horny and my body remembers exactly what he felt like last year as if it was yesterday?

I shake myself. "Do you need to come in? Use the restroom? Something?" So much for not showing him my nervousness.

He shakes his head. "I'm okay."

"I won't bite," I sass, trying to bring some humor into this situation. A bucket of water is what I need to douse the fire burning within me.

"I'm afraid I will." He chuckles, deep and throaty and hot, as he sees my eyes widen. So hot. So, so hot.

"My hands are itching to touch you and I—" with an exhale his hands slides over his lips and chin "—I would really like to take you on a date."

"Well, well, well. Asher Hunter, aren't you a gentleman?" I wink at him, and he smiles. "Give me a second to grab my purse."

I grab my purse and phone and meet Asher right outside my door at the Amelia Inn. This little town is so quaint and beautiful, and I love that I get to spend every New Year's Eve here.

Today, I'm glad I get to show Asher around. He leads us to his car, some rental according to him, my hand draped through his arm and his scent wrapping me up like a hug.

"Mmm, this is not the way," I say, pointing toward downtown, where he's driving us.

He nods but continues driving like he didn't hear me.

"You know, it's bad manners to ignore beautiful girls you're supposed to be out on a date with."

"I thought you said you were a woman." *This asshat.*

"Fair, fair."

"I want to see the lights with you before we head to dinner. I heard they're beautiful out here." He's not wrong. Amelia Island puts on beautiful lights throughout all of downtown, covering each oak tree and every store.

"Fair," I reply, breathing out and resting my head on the seat.

"Who's the one with monosyllables today?" He finally looks my way, and damn, he's breathtaking. Dark eyes pierce through me long enough that I get nervous he's going to hit something, so I tear my gaze from his.

"What's with this town and the shrimp?" He points at one of the stores, a festive shrimp with colorful lights around his neck and a Santa hat in the window.

"Don't you know about the shrimp history here?"

"Other than there's shrimp everywhere I look? No, I don't." He lowers the volume until the Christmas songs blend with the whoosh of the AC.

"Amelia Island is actually where the modern shrimping industry started. Long story short, in the early 1900s, immigrants came to Fernandina Beach. Italians, I believe, but don't quote me on that."

I twirl a piece of my hair between my fingers.

"They were the first to use powered boats and wider nets, and it changed the way the world caught shrimp. It turned Amelia Island into a shrimping town, and now all the celebrations include shrimp."

"All the celebrations?" he asks as he turns the car into the parking lot of the Ritz Carlton.

"Yeah, a shrimp festival, the shrimp drop, and who knows what else." I reach over to my door, but his hand covers mine, stopping me.

"Let me," he says, and I nod, biting my lower lip on my usual corner, a habit I can't break. In the blink of an eye, he comes around the car, almost rolling over the hood in a race to beat the valet, which he does. With my hand in his, he leads us to the room where the dinner is hosted.

I told Livie and my siblings I wasn't sitting at my usual table this year and they almost collapsed. The insufferable number of questions about why and who I was coming with were beyond what anyone could expect. And yes, one would think that after being so reserved and sticking to the same pattern like my life depended on it, I would be freaking out, but I'm not and I won't. Right? I can be spontaneous. Hell, I was spontaneous. Here I am, showing everyone, including myself, how much of a rule breaker I can be.

The dinner is a three-course meal, naturally. Nicole had a hand in organizing it—because of course she did—and since our family palate is basically the United Nations of food preferences, there's something for everyone. Variety, check.

This is also the exact type of dinner where about forty percent of my dates historically crash and burn. Not because I'm picky, but because men are either shocked I don't eat meat, like I've just confessed to being an alien, or compelled to point out that I 'have a good body,' whatever that even means. As if I should hand out Yelp reviews for unsolicited commentary on my thighs. Newsflash: both of those conversational detours are boring. Move along, sir. I eat what I eat because I want to, like everyone else.

Same with men. I know what I want. It's not being picky; it's realizing what works for me. A man who can sit across from me, not make my food choices a TED Talk, and ask questions out of curiosity, not judgment? That's what works.

Revolutionary concept, I know.

Not that this is a real date. Right?

Appetizers arrive, and not even that can break the tension between us. A whole elephant's worth of tension—365 days' worth, to be exact.

"You know you can eat whatever you want, right?" he says, eyes glued to my plate. Oh, here we go.

"I know. I love salads." I stab my fork into the house salad and take a bite, giving him a polite, closed-lipped smile.

"Good. I was just making sure. Sometimes, women play it safe on dates and eat whatever they think men want them to eat."

"Oh really? And what is it that men want us to eat?"

He throws his hands up. "Most men, not me. I want my dates to eat whatever they want and be happy. That's what makes good company, you know?" Then, he dips his spoon into his lobster bisque so effortlessly, he might as well be starring in an ad for soup.

With that face, I would buy the soup, if I ate sea creatures that is.

I nod, because, damn it, he's right. That's exactly why most of my dates implode. I don't do fake. I don't do lies. My Virgo radar spots them a mile away.

Men who think they can bluff their way into my panties? First to get benched. Which is exactly why I've been looking forward to this: he actually seems to enjoy my company. Like, beyond last year's escapade that still makes me blush if I think about it too long.

"So . . . is that what this is? A date?" I ask, because if I don't drag the hard conversation onto the table now, my brain will obsess about it all night. I overthink the smallest of things—certainly this too. Better to tackle it with overpriced wine as backup.

"It can be a date for twenty-four hours, but that's all I can give right now, Hailey." His jaw tightens as if he's eating jawbreakers.

I take a sip of wine and set the glass down. "Is this when we talk about what we're doing?"

He nods. I lean in. "Last year, this would have been so out of the realm for me, it isn't even funny. Not only will we see each other once a year, but I'm ten years older than you, Asher. Thirty-two. That's 'prime age to settle down, have kids, be a housewife' territory."

He laughs—actually laughs. "Is that what you want? Or just what you think you're supposed to want because society drilled it into you?" He sips his wine like he didn't just lob a question I think most people should frame on their walls.

And there it is.

Nobody in my life has *ever* asked me that.

Everyone just assumed I'd stick to my checklist like gospel. Career, check. Stability, check. Marriage, to be determined.

"It was . . . or I thought it was," I admit, pushing my plate away and turning to face him fully. "But the last two years have been a clusterfuck."

He gasps. "Hailey . . . you cuss?"

"Yes." The giggle that follows comes out louder than intended. A couple people look over, so I mutter an apology and take another sip. "God, I'm so loud."

He shakes his head.

"Don't apologize for taking up space. Stars are supposed to take the spotlight." He winks.

Winks.

And my face heats faster than the wine can cool it.

"Oh, I wasn't apologizing. I was warning you." I lift my glass. "You're officially with the loud girl in the red dress."

"With the prettiest eyes and the glossiest hair, you forgot to add."

"Asher Hunter, you found words in the year we've been apart," I tease, returning to my crisp wine. There's nothing Moscato can't fix.

"I saw things nobody should see, and it put everything into perspective." His somber words rest between us.

How I wish I didn't know exactly what he's referring to. I have seen so much hurt as a trauma nurse, but I can't imagine how much he's witnessed as a member of the Coast Guard. I can't fathom it, not really.

"That's actually what's been going on with me. Without adding too much trauma to this conversation, my job has taken a toll these past two years, and I'm at a crossroads on what to do. But something's gotta change, or I won't make it."

"Don't say that," he says with a bite behind his words.

"It's true. I need to think about next steps . . . so not adding a relationship to the mix actually works for me. This has been one of the things I've been looking forward to all year in the midst of chaos."

He nods. "Same."

"Elaborate." I take a bite of my cauliflower mash and sautéed carrots that they do so well every year. My mouth is so full, there's no way I'll be able to talk about anything, so it's his turn.

"Well, for starters, I live in Alaska."

My eyes widen.

"Not that there aren't women in Alaska. I'm just focused on my job right now. Kodiak's station is my dream, and I'm there now. I won't do anything to jeopardize it."

"Oh, and a girlfriend would?"

He ponders my question for a moment. "I'm an all-in kinda guy, Hales, and right now, I can only be all in at my job."

"Then what are you doing here?"

"I need hope. I need something to look forward to, and you agreeing to see me today was the light I needed to make it out of the darkness of this year. My beacon of light at sea."

I smile at him, trying to bring some comfort to this situation. "Nobody has ever called me their hope before. I'm flattered."

He tsks. "I'm serious. I'm gonna have to find some hope for this year too, and you, at the very least, are a very beautiful hope to look forward to." He blinks and smiles with his perfect, straight white teeth putting mine to shame. There's something so appealing about a man with good hygiene in general, but good teeth? Yes, please.

"At the risk of sounding needy, we can do this again if you want."

"I can't stop you from finding a partner, Hailey. I appreciate you holding out for a year to meet me here, but I can't do that again, and I can't offer you companionship."

"Who says I held out for a year?" I arch an eyebrow, pretending to radiate the confidence I definitely don't feel.

"You being here with me . . . or do you have a boyfriend back home?"

I laugh lightly, shaking my head. "Relax. I was kidding. No boyfriend. I haven't met anyone, and I'm open too. I'm fine keeping this . . . arrangement. If we don't meet anyone else, we can still see each other in a year."

It sounds reasonable in theory, but I already know it's a ridiculous plan. A practical person would cut their losses, not cling to someone they've only seen *twice*.

No.

Three times. A *very* practical person would get to know this man better before making pacts like some lovesick Jane Austen character.

"I do have one condition, though."

He crosses his leg over his knee, and my eyes betray me by darting straight to his lap. Not my proudest moment. I remember *exactly* what's there.

"I'm listening," he says, snapping me out of my thoughts.

"No celibacy clause," I declare firmly, like I'm laying down constitutional law.

"We both have needs. I refuse to spend eleven months repressing mine just because I'm waiting to hang out with you. That's unhealthy."

"Agreed," he replies instantly. Bless rational men.

"Good. And . . . we actually get to know each other. Friendship, maybe. Connection, sure. I practically levitated when I got your letter, so clearly, there's something here worth exploring beyond, you know, your physical anatomy." My smile carries all the meaning I'm implying.

He nods. "I love letters. That sounds good."

I blink. "We have texting. FaceTime. We're not in the nineteen-hundreds you know?"

He tips his head, hand brushing his perfectly trimmed beard, studying me like I'm an exhibit at a museum. "I do love letters. My parents never allowed mail. They even opened the letters from my teachers. So as soon as I became an adult—"

"You're barely an adult," I cut in, biting my lip. My smile is smug but warm.

He smirks. "I sure as hell fucked you like one, didn't I?"

My jaw drops. No witty retort. Nothing.

Okay, then, Ash.

"As I was saying," he continues smoothly, "letters matter to me. If it's okay with you, I'd love that. In the fall, we can decide if we want to see each other again."

"Fine." I nod briskly, regaining some composure. "As long as Nicole keeps throwing this gala, I'll be here. I can't exactly fly to you during the holidays."

"Hailey, I live on an island that's freezing cold almost two hundred days of the year. I get called to rescue people from the Bering Sea at all hours. I would *love* for you to stay as far away from it as possible."

"Freezing. Dangerous. Noted."

"It's beautiful, don't get me wrong, but I associate Kodiak with work, with the relentless waves. I'd like to keep you separate from that. I respect both you and her the same, but her, I fear. You, I crave."

His words bring shivers down my spine. "Her?"

"The Bering."

"The sea is a girl? Color me shocked."

"In Spanish, the word for sea uses a masculine article, el mar, but I've always thought about it as a girl. Female rage and all."

He stands, offering me his hand. I take it, following him toward the ballroom. Conversation: tabled.

"Letters it is, then," I murmur. "Very vintage of us."

"Hi, hi, hi!" Livie comes barreling toward us, dragging her husband along. The moment I dreaded. How the hell do I introduce him? Annual hook-up? Lifetime mistake in progress? But I don't make reckless decisions, right? I live my carefully crafted life always to avoid them. So this? I don't know what to call it.

"This is my friend," I say finally, forcing a smile.

"Asher," he says warmly, extending his hand.

"Livie," she replies, eyeing him up and down like she's sizing up a suspect. At barely five feet tall, she looks ridiculous facing off against a giant, and I burst into laughter.

"So who are you, Asher? You look familiar."

"I'm a friend of Hailey's." His tone is confident, and if it wasn't for Livie knowing my whole damn life, it would've been believable.

"Hailey doesn't have any friends I don't know." Exactly my point. I roll my eyes at her.

"Liv!" I hiss, glaring.

"It's fine," he chuckles. "We met briefly a couple years ago. I think I was even wearing this same outfit. Guilty."

That smile of his—equal parts charming and sinful—could melt an iceberg. Maybe that's why he likes working in frigid waters. Somehow, he can stay warm with his damn charm.

"How briefly?" Livie presses, hands on hips.

"At the shrimp drop. For like a split second." His jaw clenches as he fights back laughter.

Livie's eyes widen. She tugs Alex closer. "It's *him*! She didn't make him up!"

"You told your friends about me?" Asher murmurs in my ear.

"Two years ago, when I was convinced you were imaginary, yes."

"And now you're, what? Dating?" Livie demands.

"No," we both say in unison.

"I'm confused."

"I'll let you take this one," Asher says smoothly, stepping behind me like I'm the official spokesperson for . . . whatever this is.

I let out a breath. "We're friends. That's all. New friends, if you will."

Livie looks at us skeptically but doesn't say anything as her husband says, "Come on, shortie. Let them be. You and I should give them some space, yeah?"

She considers him but eventually lets out a defeated breath. "Fine!" Her fingers go up to her eyes, and she mimics pointing them at Asher. "I'm keeping my eyes on you, though. Be nice to my girl."

"Only way I know how to be," he mentions, kissing the top of my head and making me stand straighter.

That little act of affection will be the death of me. *The death of me.*

"As we were saying." I turn around and land on his chest as he sways us to whatever song is playing. "When do we stop this? Us?"

"When one of us feels like it. Either this stops serving us, or we want more than what the other person could give," he declares. "Our relationship—"

"Is this what this is?" I interrupt.

He pinches his nose but doesn't stop swaying us. "It is a relationship. A relationship is a way two things are connected. In our case, two people. We have a purpose, maintain a friendship at a distance, offer companionship, and enjoy our company once a year. One could call it a contract, if you think about it."

"A contract. So sexy." It comes out of my mouth playfully, but I believe in the truth behind those words wholeheartedly. Clear boundaries and guidelines are sexy. They are hot.

"Isn't that what marriage is? A legal binding document for a relationship?" When you think about it that way, I guess it is. I nod. "Except I'm not asking to marry you. I'm asking that if the stars align and the seasons change, we keep this up for as long as it serves us both."

This was not on my to do list, but I can't deny myself the pleasure or how easy this fits into my current everyday life. I could stand, or dance here, I guess, overthinking every one of these words, dissecting his proposal to see if there's a way we can perfect it even more, but really, this sounds as productive as anything else could be right now. And maybe knowing I will have his body every year will appease my brain a little more in the in-betweens. Maybe I'll stop craving him as much as I did this year. If there's something I'm good at, it's controlling a situation. He's allowing me to control all the variables here, and I like it.

"Sounds like a plan," I agree. He twirls me around and continues dancing with me until my feet hurt, until we double over from laughing and getting to know each other little by little. In between learning his favorite color is black like his soul or that he only feels alive at sea, I've found I like Asher Hunter and all the parts of himself he shares. Even more than I liked getting into bed with him last year.

The shrimp drop passes, and after hugging everyone and their mother, we leave the gala with our bellies and our hearts full, our heads spinning from fizzy drinks and wine. At least mine are. I don't remember the last time he actually drank anything other than water. We drive down the street until he's parked at the beach parking lot. He steps out of the car, running to my side before I can open the door.

"I can open my own doors, Ash," I all but groan. His thick, dark brows furrow as he stands there with no shoes, in just his shirt and pants. "When did you take your shoes off?"

"In the past five minutes, when we were just sitting here in the parking lot and you were busy rambling about the decline of grammar in text messages." We both chuckle. Okay, I might be a little tipsy. "And I know you *can* open your own doors, but you should let me open them for you. You should let me do my job."

"This is 2028 now, Asher. Fuck the patriarchy!" I shout at the top of my lungs.

"You allowing me to take care of you is not embracing the patriarchy. You can be a feminist and allow others to take care of you."

His eyes are dark and enticing and perfect, and I want to take them home with me.

"I don't know who fucked with your brain so much that you think if you're not the one taking care of people all the time, it will break you."

"I never said anything of the sort," I fight back.

He shakes his head and chuckles. "You didn't have to. It's obvious, especially after everything you said today."

"Explain." I cross my arms over my chest as a loud hiccup escapes my lips.

Asher smiles at that. "That was cute."

I roll my eyes and cover my mouth with my hands, as if it will do anything to contain the roar that comes out when I hiccup again. I'm a lion now, got it.

"Come on, let's go for a walk, and I'll tell you."

"It's so cold!" I shout, all but pouting. He clears his throat, guiding my gaze to his hands holding his jacket, and I shrug. I step out, allowing him to slide the jacket on, and I immediately moan with my eyes closed. He smells salty and musky, a mix between smoky wood and the sea. It blends perfectly with the crash of the waves and the distant shouts of people still celebrating the New Year.

"This smells delicious," I mutter, his deep chuckle shaking me awake.

"Get over yourself. We already knew you had good taste. Look at me." I turn around, showing him my body and almost falling from everything spinning.

"Come on, Hales. Let's go for a walk."

"I love that you call me that," I whisper against his chest as he drapes an arm around me and walks us toward the water. I'm dragging my feet through the sand and cringing at the feel. Unfortunately for me and everyone around me who loves the beach, I hate the sand. I *hate* it. With a passion. But I'm also not going to act like a spoiled, high maintenance girl, so here I am. I also dislike spontaneous shit. If he would've told me we were going to do this, I would have prepared and brought different shoes.

The cool breeze caresses my cheeks, and I hope it cools me down from the outside in. Not enough for him not to notice something is bothering me, though. "What's wrong?" he asks, stopping in his tracks.

"Nothing." I try to keep walking, but he pulls me back, pinning me between his chest and his arm.

"I don't know if you know this, but you're a bad liar, Hales."

"I hate lies." I'd rather be hurt with the truth than stand in comfort with a lie that will remove the rug from under me later.

"That is true. So let's try that again. What's wrong?" he asks, searching my eyes. He doesn't seem annoyed and truly doesn't seem like it's bothering him that something is bugging me. I'm not usually one for needing things to be fixed. I'm usually the fixer in the group, the one who takes other's problems as my own and then wonders why the hell I'm so exhausted all the time. It's taxing. But Asher asking me what's bothering me and not taking a no for an answer might be my new Holy Grail.

"I hate the sand," I finally say with an exasperated breath. "These shoes don't really scream *walk in the sand after dancing and drinking for hours* and I—ah!"

I'm upside down.

I'm over his shoulder, ass in the air, completely upside down.

"What are you doing?" I try to kick my feet, but it's in vain, because he's solid as a rock and damn strong too.

"You don't like the sand. Not a problem." He keeps walking toward the water.

"I'm not going swimming in that cold ass water, Asher Hunter."

He chuckles and carries on.

"I'm serious, Asher. Do not put me in that water." I can't see how far from the water we are. That's partially because it's dark; there are no lights allowed at night on Amelia Island because they disrupt the sea turtles nesting and navigation. Plus, his giant body is blocking the view. I'm still bouncing on his shoulders like he is a damn roller-coaster. When I said I wanted to ride him, this is not what I meant.

"You don't need to know how to swim. I can rescue you, remember?" The waves sound a lot closer, and I'm about to lose my shit on this man.

"Put me down!" I shout again, and maybe it's the anger behind my words that does it, but he stops and slides me down—softly, easily, tenderly. Not to the sand, but to his feet. It's so controlled, it feels like he does it in slow motion. I'm acutely aware of how close we are to each other, and my little pent up breaths remind me entirely of our time last year. Reminds my clit too.

"I don't want to get in the water," I declare.

He nods, hearing the seriousness behind my tone. He knows I'm not playing, and I like that he's taking his time to respect it. "Why?"

"Because it's dark, and cold, and we didn't plan for this."

"It is dark, I'll give you that. But it's not that cold in Florida, and you're right, we didn't plan for this." He rakes his fingers through my hair, detangling it as he slides them down. "Do you always live your life like this? With thoughtfully designed plans?"

"What do you mean?" I play coy. I have to, because how is this man seeing directly into my soul? Into my biggest weakness? Into my biggest flaw?

Without a plan, everything fails.

I was called rigid for so long growing up, and I can't shake it. It's the only way for me to control my life as much as I can: by making plans and sticking to them. Hell, actually, Asher has been the biggest surprise in my life yet. Maybe that's why I'm so frazzled by him half the time.

"Do you always need to plan for things? Is that why you wanted us to lay our relationship out in the open? For you to know the plan?"

I nod and look at his dark eyes, hoping he can see the vulnerability I'm about to share. "I like to know what to expect," I reply.

"From what?" he asks, his hand sliding up my back slowly between his jacket and my dress, leaving goosebumps and want in its wake.

"Life." I let out a breathy sound. His fingers knead at my nape while his other hand rests on my lower back comfortably, holding me in place. Good thing he is, because I feel like I could melt at any given time and become slush by the shore instead.

"Don't you know the best things in life come unexpectedly?" His words are like the hug I didn't know I needed, like a sledgehammer trying to break down my walls.

"Yeah, but there's no success in the unexpected," I add.

He nods as if he understands. "Life without success is not a life I want. I get it." He lets out a breath. "I get it more than you may realize, but we can't walk around like life's a tight rope that can't bend or mold when needed."

I shrug. Says who? Because I can. I definitely have.

"That's when you snap, Hales."

I let his words hang between us. I can't take them right now. Right now, the only thing keeping me afloat is pulling that rope as tight as I can, or I'm going under. Work, my family's struggles, my loneliness, all of it—it's too much, and I need to be careful so I don't sink deeper with them. I need to be careful so I don't drown. So, if my plans are the rope keeping me alive, I'm holding on to it with both hands.

"I thought holding tight makes you stronger." I finally move my hands, sliding them up his hard chest and holding his face with both hands.

"It can also break your hands, baby."

"Baby?" I savor the name on my lips; I like it a whole lot more than I should for someone who's about to not see this man again for another whole year.

"Is that out of your plans? Me calling you *baby?*" he asks, lowering his face to my lips.

"You can mess up my plans anytime, Asher Hunter. Apparently, that's your M.O., no?" His lips are so close to mine. So close, I can smell fresh peppermint. So close, I can almost feel his softness on my own. So close, I shut my eyes so he can just kiss me and I can get lost in him. But he doesn't. Instead, he picks me up by my ass and breaks into a sprint.

"No!" I shout, but it's too late. I'm being turned and going quicker than I expected, plunging horizontally into the water on top of him.

The water is frigid and salty and not deep at all. His body is barely submerged, so only my breasts and feet are underwater. I think I made it safely, and I can get away from his hold, but he continues walking backwards like a crab, going deeper and deeper. I yelp and wrap my legs around his ass. I hate everything about this. All of it.

His face pops out of the water, and he smiles wickedly at me. "You said I could mess up your plans, baby. This is me coming at them like a wrecking ball."

"I actually hate this!" I shout, tensing even more in his hands as I'm submerged into the water. It's so fucking cold, I'm going to lose my shit.

"It's so cold!" I shout, but he doesn't listen. He keeps going deeper and deeper until he sits up, half our bodies underwater. I breathe heavily where, for him, this is child's play. He's so calm, almost as if they are one, the ocean and him.

"I told you I didn't want to come in!" I shout, smacking him playfully with my hand.

"And you also said I could wreck your plans. This is me doing that. Live a little, Hailey. Life's too short."

I guess he's right. Life *is* too short, but I hate this.

"This dress was so expensive." It's the only thing that comes out of my lips as I start relaxing against him. Now that my body is starting to get used to the temperature, maybe I can relax. That's if I don't think too much about all the creatures that might be under us right now. The thought of that alone makes me shiver.

"You said so two years ago."

"And you dismissed it and still dunked us in this water?" I splash his way, and he smiles. Not flinching, not closing his eyes, he smiles. Fucking ocean cowboy, acting all tough when he's near the water and making me want to do wild things out here in the open with his wicked smile, perfect mustache, and pretty eyes. Pretty eyes hiding behind almost foggy glasses. I lift them up, letting them rest at the top of his head and keeping my hand wrapped around his neck.

"I'd buy you another dress just to get your legs wrapped around me just like this." His gaze drops to my lips. "If I could keep you clinging to me as if I'm your anchor, baby, I'd buy you three."

I roll my eyes. "So cheesy."

He shrugs. "Maybe. But you liked it."

"I did not," I tease.

He moves my bangs away from my face and stares into my eyes. "Your eyes are so damn beautiful, Hailey. I've never seen anything like them."

"They're kind of soulless."

"If you think that, your mirror must be broken." His gaze bounces between my eyes as he holds my face.

"Your eyes are like a door to a home. Not to a house, but a home. They bring others comfort. It's like as long as I'm looking at you, I know I'm not lost."

I suck in a breath, but he doesn't let me speak before he continues. "It sounds a little fatuous, but it's true. I dreamed about them for entirely too long these past two years. I wish I would have just taken a picture, because my memory didn't do them justice."

This is too much, too many compliments all at once, and what am I supposed to say? So instead, I close the tiny space between us and kiss him.

His lips are full and wet. They taste like mint and sea salt, and they touch mine effortlessly, just like he dances. Just like he talks.

His lips leave a tingling sensation behind and heat surging through my body, warming me up completely.

Cold water where? Not here, where his dick grows hard and my insides are on fire. A single kiss, and I'm bursting.

I'm unraveling in his arms with his lips on mine, and I don't want this to end. For a split second, as he licks and kisses and sucks my tongue into his mouth, I forget we're in the water, I forget he leaves tonight, forget I won't see him again. I allow myself to forget it all and just kiss him.

His hands squeeze my ass, lifting me slightly. In another life, Hailey wouldn't even consider letting him have his way with me here, but in this life, Hailey is all for this living in the moment shit.

I slide his hand up my ass and over my sex, right where I want him to touch. Right where I want him to make me feel it all. He smiles against my mouth, and I bite his lower lip.

"Do you want to get out of here?" he asks.

"I think I might die if you don't make me come in the next three minutes," I sass, hoping it will earn me one of his deep chuckles . . . and it does.

"I don't need three minutes to make you come." With those words, he slides his fingers against my clit, and I hiss at the contact. All the pent up angst and want from months are right at the surface. I'm so needy and ready to combust; he's right: it won't take me long.

He peppers kisses down my neck, urging me up with his hand so my breast lands near his mouth. He opens and takes all of me into it, biting gently and pulling a moan from my lips. I yank at the fabric, and with a tearing sound, I pull it over my breast, giving him full access.

"I thought this was an expensive dress," he says against my nipple, making it harden immediately. Balancing on my knees with his fingers buried inside me with the waves crashing on shore moving us side to side proves to either be harder than a work out, or I'm extremely out of shape.

"I thought you said you could buy me three of them."

"Fuck the dress," he says, lowering the fabric further and bringing his lips to my nipple. My back arches against his touch, welcoming his tongue and his teeth as he licks and bites the sensitive skin.

I grind against his hand and pull his head closer to me. I'm chasing this with all I have, because I want to feel good with his touch. I want to feel good with his mouth on me. I want to come undone, right here, and I want him to do it. *Now.*

He bites my nipple hard, the sting making me hiss, but he immediately sucks it into his mouth, soothing the pain. He slides another finger in, stuffing me so full but allowing a few seconds for me to stretch around them before pumping in and out. I pull my dress down over my other breast, a wordless invitation for him to give the attention it needs.

I look down at him, at this man smiling up at me, the lust behind his eyes not lost on me. I feel so powerful under his touch, like I can do it all when he looks at me this way.

"I love that you're so needy for me," he says, crawling his lips to my other breast and showing me the red mark on the other one. I can barely see anything with just the moon and the distant fireworks illuminating the space, but I can definitely see the bite marks and the small spots that will surely bruise tomorrow.

"And I thought you were going to make me come in less than three minutes."

I see it, the moment it clicks. The hunger, the lust, the want, the *need* to stay true to his words. His mouth lowers to my other nipple, and he repeats the same process. Kissing, licking, biting, sucking my entire breast while pumping his fingers in and out. I'm so close, but this feels so good, I want it to last forever.

"Let go, Hailey," he whispers against my breast, and I shake my head. He bites on my nipple harder.

"Asher!" I scream his name, so loud, I'm sure every single beach house heard it. He licks my nipple again, and I hiss but won't let go. I squeeze my inner walls tighter, and he groans against my skin. I want his dick so bad—his fingers are not going to make it work.

"I know you want my dick baby, I feel you trying to tease it, but my condoms are in the car, and I won't fuck you bare." Our eyes clash, the need, lust, and want mirroring each other. "Not like this. So please, give it to me so we can go to the hotel room and I can fuck that sassy mouth and your tight little cunt."

I gasp. God, he knows my body so well. He's either a fucking expert, or I'm easier to read than an open book.

"Tell me what will do it." His breathing is as erratic as mine, like he's desperate to make me come. "You look so pretty when you come, and with the stars above us and surrounded by my favorite thing, I want to see it again."

"Touch my clit while you bite me," I whisper. Fuck, I've never openly asked for what I want before, but damn, if it doesn't feel good. His eyes widen before he dives, mouth first, into my neck, biting hard like a damn ocean cowboy vampire.

"Yes," I moan, breathy and needy and *his*.

He shifts his hand, his thumb pressing against my clit while three of his fingers stretch me. He moves them in and out in a curve, touching a spot that makes my entire body shake. And then, he bites my nipple; it hurts so fucking bad that it feels good. I pull gently at his hair and come down from my high right on his hand.

"Aaaaash," I breathe out before his lips cover mine and he kisses me senseless. He kisses me hard, biting and licking, until I can taste blood between our tongues. I moan, coming again on his hand. He groans, not letting go of the pleasure spot and sucking my bloody lip into his mouth.

I breathe out, moving my body slowly against his. My hands drop to his chest as he lets go of my lips and slides his fingers out.

"You're so beautiful," he whispers, holding my face and smiling at me.

"Thanks."

The word is broken and breathy, and all I want to do now is take a nap. He fixes my dress—as much as he can, I guess—and carries me out of the water into the car. The drive to the hotel is eternal, even if it's only two minutes long. Having a wet dress will definitely do that to a girl, but it's all worth it. Because as soon as we get to the room, he does his words justice and fucks me into oblivion.

FEBRUARY, 2028

Dear Asher:

Six weeks since I saw you. I can't believe we're doing this, but I guess we are. Things at work are hard. I hate it, and I've never hated work. It's one of the things that makes me good at it. That I can usually find the light even in the darkest night (see me using your metaphor here?)

It's Valentine's day this weekend, and I'm on call. On purpose, that is, because what else am I going to do? I don't know how much about my personal life you actually want to know; if it's TMI, just tell me.

The dating pool in Baker Oaks is smaller than ever, and I don't have the energy or the bandwidth to do anything after work most days. My free time usually goes to helping at home. Since my mother's Multiple Sclerosis diagnosis, I've been picking up more and more things there. This, I don't want to talk too much about, so you only get one question.

Livie and Alex are trying to have a baby but having trouble. It hurts my heart seeing her cry every month when she gets her period, so a lot of my free time has gone to just cheering her up. I'm *picking up extra shifts here and there, trying to pay off all my student loans so I can pitch in with my mom's treatments a little more. All of it is exhausting, which leaves me with little desire to date or try to meet someone outside this town.*

My job, well, I hate it. Just thinking about it makes me mad. I used to love being a trauma nurse at the pediatric hospital, but I've been doing it for over a decade, and I guess seeing children hurting and dying eventually takes a toll on your own mental health. I don't know how much longer I can do this.

I'm sorry if I'm being a whiny baby, but I can't share all of this with Livie or my sisters. They're going through so much already. Everyone at work either loves it, or they're new, and well, I guess I'm a loner now. I don't have anyone else in my life but the guy I'm only able to see once a year and I can't even call.

Please tell me something funny. Anything. Bring some light into my life again.

Oh, by the way, here's my phone number: 904-852-9633. I know you said you liked letters, but just in case you needed it for whatever reason.

Xo,
Hales

MARCH, 2028

Dear Hailey:

Happy late Valentine's Day. I'm sorry you had to work and you didn't have anyone to celebrate with. You asked for something funny, but my life is anything but right now. So how about a joke?

How do vampires know if they had a successful Valentine's Day?

Try to answer.

Don't look yet.

Try again.

Ok, now read the answer.

If it's love at first bite.

I hope it made you laugh, even if just a little bit.

I'm so sorry you hate work. Nobody should be tied down doing something for hours every day that they don't love. Because then, you're basically working twice: once for the actual grind and again to fake a smile that says, "Yeah, this is totally fine and not soul-crushing at all." Maybe there's another department you could slide *into? Or maybe you've got some hidden talent you can freelance? I'd give you more solid advice, but the only thing I did before this was sling fries and mop floors at a fast-food joint, which, trust me, was far less heroic than what I do now.*

Being an AST is a whole different world. I love it. I mean, where else do you get paid to jump out of helicopters into freezing water, drag people back from the edge of disaster, and then still have time to hit the gym afterward? It's like James Bond meets Baywatch, minus the slow-motion hair flips. (Did that make you smile? I hope it did, because I worked hard to come up with that line).

But it's not just about the thrill. I love the brotherhood, the purpose, the fact that when things get rough, I'm the one who gets to step up. My life growing up was sad and hard. I wouldn't wish it on anyone, and maybe one day, I'll tell you all about it. I felt useless most of the time. If I wasn't the best, I might as well not even come home. So, I learned to be the best at everything. Grades, sports, cleaning my room, doing chores, staying quiet, all of it. I was so good at the latter, most of the time, they didn't even know if I was right there in front of them. It didn't matter that I graduated with honors or that I was captain of several teams, including swimming. It was never celebrated. But here, in this place, I am. Here, I'm valued. Here, I matter.

When that call comes in, it's not about clocking hours—it's about someone's life depending on me, and that makes every swim, every lift, every grueling workout worth it. And yeah, it's tough, but it's the good kind of tough that makes you proud to collapse into bed knowing you did something that actually mattered.

This job made me realize the love I chased for so long from my parents wasn't really needed. It's not love I need to thrive; it's appreciation, and here I am, appreciated. Are you appreciated at work? Maybe go somewhere where you are, and the load will feel less heavy?

The problem with that is I find myself working more than I'm needed, always chasing the validation I'm given. It's like a drug, Hales, and I'm addicted. It definitely doesn't give me time for much, but it fuels my soul in a way nothing ever has before.

Well, this turned sad, didn't it? How about another joke?

What's a race that is never run?

Think about it.

Don't look.

Think about it.

Ok, now.

A swimming race.

Funny? Maybe not, but my dad wasn't one for dad jokes, so I had to learn them myself.

It's about to be busy season. The closer it gets to warmer weather, the more tourists come and the more we have to go rescue them. So, if you don't hear from me frequently, that's why.

I was also thinking about sharing something special with you, more than what I've already shared, that is. I don't usually talk to people about anything important, and I just gave you my whole life story within these pages. I hope you don't sell them for profit or anything one day when I'm a hero.

If I share more secrets with you, can you keep them safe? Can you be my treasure chest, Hailey?

I'm going to assume your answer is yes and tell you anyway.

I only wear fuzzy socks. I don't like the texture of the rest of them. Another point for loving Alaska—my feet aren't sweating when I'm wearing miniature sweaters on them.

With kindness,

Ash

JUNE, 2028

Dear Asher:

Time is a figment of the imagination, because there's no way it's been six months since I last saw you. I don't know if it's because I reread your letters over and over again to feel close to you or the fact that I stalk your social media to see what you're up to. I'm such a loser, aren't I? Finding comfort in a man a bazillion miles away from me who jumps into ice cold waters for a living and who I'm definitely not dating.

I've loved all your little random facts; have I told you that before? I swear, I'm losing my mind lately. I can't remember day from night or right from wrong. I'm so tired all the time, I'm afraid I'll make a mistake somewhere, especially at work. So forgive me if I've said that before.

Update on me. I got one of those new phones with the hologram, and I feel very Zenon-like. I kind of wish cars flew by now, but I'll take cool phones in their place.

Nicole, my baby sister who organizes the gala, is getting married, and I'm so excited for her. She's joining the rest of them in the married-before-thirty club. And then, there's me, the oldest, still childless and single. I guess at this point, it's comical. I should just cut my losses and find a different dream.

Thank you for the jokes. They've been great, especially on days when I'm struggling to find some joy. I'll share it with the kids at work—they'll love it. Some days, I laugh at myself over the fact that my closest friendship is with you, and I don't even know your favorite song or why you love swimming so much.

I have a joke today. I farted at work.

Yup, you read that right.

I farted.

A big, loud fart.

Why? Well, there was a little nine year old crying over missing her sibling, who was in surgery, and I didn't know what else to do. She laughed and then I laughed, and all was fine.

It was embarrassing, but it brought me life. Maybe that's what we both need to do— fart more.

Xo,
Hales

SEPTEMBER, 2028

Dear Asher:

Did my fart spook you? It did, didn't it? I realized it after weeks of not getting another letter. I know you're only twenty-three, and you might think girls are all glitter and spice, but I'll let you in on a secret: everyone farts.

Everybody poops too.

Most women bleed through their vagina.

And I'm done being weird now.

I'm writing this tipsy.

Tipsy and alone.

This was another month of me being everyone's mom. Livie's confidant and pillow to cry on. My mother's medical jargon translator. The best maid of honor a girl could ask for, driving around town for hours until Nicole found her favorite dress. She looks stunning, and she will be a beautiful bride soon. I got promoted at work. Yay, right? Wrong! It comes with more responsibilities, and now, I'm mentoring new nurses. They're so sweet and innocent and full of light, and I just don't have any in me to give them anymore. I feel like I'm tainting them with my perspective, and that makes me feel even worse.

That's my recap. I sound absolutely insufferable, and I might understand if you just want our friendship to end.

I do need to know before I buy tickets for the gala this year: are you still interested in coming along, or did you find a woman to love?

Let me know either way,

Xo,

Hales

OCTOBER, 2028

Dear Hailey,

I'm sorry I disappeared. In April, there was a vessel that went down at the end of the season when we thought we wouldn't have to worry about large crews out there. We were wrong. We were out for days, and we lost many of them. I know it's not necessarily the news you were hoping for, but that's why I stopped writing. I didn't know how hard it would hit me to fail miserably at a mission like that.

I'm in a better headspace now, so I'm writing back. You could never spook me with farts or anything else—actually, that made me laugh out loud. Thank you for that. I needed it. Sorry if you thought I was avoiding you. It was more that I didn't have anything to give those months, so I just didn't reach out. I almost called you, though. I just wanted to hear your voice, but I had nothing to say. I don't think I ever gave you my number, so here it is: 907-859-7412. Just for emergencies, though. I still want my letters.

I'm still planning on going to the gala. I have leave for a few extra days, so I will be around after, if you'd like to hang out for longer. *Either way is fine by me. And if you've found a date, that's okay too.*

Are you celebrating Halloween? If so, what are you dressing up as?

How about another joke?

Why wouldn't the ghost dance at the party?

Think about it.

No peeking.

Really, I should just not tell you.

See you in a couple months.

With kindness,

Asher

P.S. Because he had no body to dance with.

Dear Asher,

I'm sorry to hear about the shipwreck. That's awful. I hope you know you did your best. I don't even need to know details to know you did. Just for the record, you could've called. You don't need to be at your best to be a good friend. After all, I've been a damn mess for a year, longer really, and you're still here. Or are you only here because I'm a good lay?

I'm really looking forward to seeing you next month.

That's all I have for now really.

Xo,

Hales

P.S. The ghost joke has been my favorite so far.

4

NEW YEARS EVE 2028

Breakaway by Kelly Clarkson
  &
Getaway Car by Taylor Swift

ASHER

> H:
>
> Are you in town yet?
>
> H:
>
> change of plans.
>
> H:
>
> come to my house instead of the hotel. 85345 N Yellow Pine Cir
>
> H:
>
> you know what? Never mind.

ME:

> I just got off the plane. Yes, I can go there instead. Be there in 30.

H:

It's fine. Really. No need to worry.

ME:

Hailey . . . I'm coming.

H:

sigh.

H:

fine.

H:

see you soon.

THE DRIVE to her place takes about the same time as from the Jacksonville airport to Amelia Island but in the opposite direction. I knew she lived elsewhere, but I didn't think it was this close. Maybe I should have researched a little more. The blue sign on the road welcomes me to Baker Oaks, and in no time, the taxi is pulling up to a quaint, green house featuring a small porch with two white wooden rocking chairs. There's a beautiful wreath with gold and silver stars decorating the door and a large doormat that says, "Did you bring food for my bird?"

How is it that I've known Hailey for three years, and I didn't know she had a bird? I chuckle at myself; of course I don't know everything about the girl I've seen and kissed three times. Sure, we've fucked twice, and she also happens to be my pen pal . . . but why does it feel more nauseating than the first time I jumped from a helicopter to think about knocking on her door?

"Is this it?" the driver says. Fuck, the taxi.

"Yes, here. Thank you." I pass him a tip and get out, carrying my bags all the way to the door.

Taking a deep breath, I knock on her door and wait for the nausea to subside, just like it always does when I enter the water after jumping headfirst. Is this what I'm doing here? Jumping into deep waters without knowing if I'll be able to keep us both afloat?

The door opens, and I let out a laugh—though Little Miss Sass crosses her arms and doesn't laugh with me.

"What's so funny?" she asks, but how do I tell her she looks like a mix between Kim Possible and Mrs. Incredible right now without offending her?

"Did they change the theme for the gala tonight to SWAT attire?" I try to contain my laughter but fail miserably.

"Oh, this?" She rakes her hands over her body. "We have a mission before the gala, and I thought you'd be the perfect person for it, considering you rescue people for a living."

"What?" I ask her, utterly confused.

"Get with the program, Ash. Come on!" Her little feet stomp the opposite way, disappearing into the house and carrying short, exasperated sounds with her. Damn, she's cute.

Stepping into her home is like a slap in the face. It's one hundred percent like I expected it to be, but somehow the opposite too.

It's tidy.

Beyond tidy.

Everything has a place, and I can tell just after stepping through the foyer covered in books. The long corridor takes me to where she stands in the middle of a white and sage green kitchen. Everything matches—except the collection of assorted mugs in the coffee station.

Even the open cage in the back with a beautiful bird on top of it is tidy.

She must catch me staring, because she says, "That's Bijoux. She's friendly, but we don't have time. Do you want coffee? I can make some to go."

"To go? Where are we going?" I'm sure I look puzzled, because she gives me her *I'm annoyed* look.

"We need to rescue the birds, so get dressed and don't wear anything flashy."

Maybe it's not having any self-preservation, or maybe it's the fact that she's haunted my every interaction for the past year, but I don't ask. I just do as I'm told. I let my bag fall to the floor and remove my shirt with one hand.

Hailey stops pacing and opens her gray eyes wide. "What are you doing? We have to go!"

"Changing into a darker shirt so I can match your freak." I smile, and she rolls her eyes.

"Sometimes, I forget you're so young. Match my freak? Is that what young people say nowadays?" She points down the hall to a closed door.

"That's the guest room if you want to change. I know you said you had extra days off, and I don't know if you have any plans, but that room has your name written all over it if you want to crash here."

Have I just been friend-zoned? Is this what happens when you connect with someone beyond the physical? A year of sending letters to each other, and now, she just wants me to sleep somewhere else? Maybe I shouldn't have assumed we would share a bed, but after last year's sex marathon, I assumed it would be the same. I'll take it, though. I'd take anything she's willing to give me like the touch-starved puppy I am.

A black t-shirt on, a piece of gum in my mouth, and a quick look in the mirror to make sure I don't look as tired as I feel, and I step out of the room. Hailey's still dressed in a tight, long-sleeved shirt practically painted to her body, same as her pants, all in black matching the beanie on her head. Her long hair has loose waves bouncing on top of her breasts as she paces up and down the kitchen. I walk to her, and when she sees me, she tries to walk past me, but I grab her hand, stopping her. I take both her hands in mine and bring them to my lips, kissing them softly before lowering them to my chest.

The air between us is charged with electricity, and I'm glad. So glad. The connection, the inexplicable string tying us together, is still here and intact.

It's terrifying to know that seeing each other just three times in three years and barely knowing each other means nothing when it feels like this. Like the Earth exploded and the ocean split in half. Like there's no sound, no time, no space. Like there's only me and her. People write books about feelings like this. *Does she feel this too?*

"Hales."

"Ash," she whispers in that tone I hear in my dreams.

"I will do whatever you want me to do, but unless someone's dying, I need you to explain what's going on." I pause and search her face for answers I don't find. "I need to know the situation at hand before I go into it. Whatever it is, you've got me, but I need you to communicate, okay?"

She nods and lets out a breath. "My mom's neighbor has bird contraband."

I open and close my mouth, turning my head to the side and ask, "What?"

"Oh my God, Asher Hunter. For real?" she giggles. Good, this is what I want to see. This girl is always so worked up, but at least this giggle tells me she is relaxing, even if just a little.

"For real. Elaborate."

"Can I just tell you in the car? We have a ten minute drive, and we need to go before she's back home. I'll explain then, okay?"

I nod, and she pops up on her tip toes to kiss me quickly on my lips. "Thank you for coming. I know you're probably tired from traveling."

I nod again. "I'm never too tired for you. Come on. I want to know about the lady and the birds."

Hailey grunts and hands me her keys. I follow her outside, and we head out in her navy van that somehow screams soccer mom and Hailey at the same time.

"SO LET me get this straight: your mom's neighbor has been adopting birds to resell on the black market? And you're stealing all the birds and taking them back to the rescue center?"

She nods.

"And you're doing this instead of calling the police because you don't want your mother, who has adopted birds from her in the past, to get in trouble too?"

She nods again, pulling up to a white, Victorian style, two story house with porch decoration similar to hers.

"You're a fast learner." She tries to open her door, but I hold her hand, stopping her. I narrow my eyes at her, and she shrugs.

"You can't get angry at me for forgetting I'm in the presence of a gentleman when I only see you once a year. Also, we need to hurry so shh."

I pinch the bridge of my nose and just grunt. No reason to argue with her about this. We follow a path around the side of the house, past a row of bushes that look like they've given up on life entirely but are still greener than anything you find near me this time of year.

Hailey tiptoes like she's watched too many murder mysteries and is trying not to get caught. "Is there anyone here?" I ask in hushed tones.

"No. That's why we need to hurry up." I try to mimic her but end up stepping on every crunchy leaf within a mile radius. Subtlety has never been my strength. She gives me a look, one eyebrow raised, and I pretend I meant to do it.

Classic distraction technique. Works about zero percent of the time.

We reach the back porch, where the paint is peeling in long strips that flap against the wood like old bookmarks. Hailey crouches, fiddling with the screen door lock, her tongue poking out of the corner of her mouth in concentration. I don't know why that tiny quirk makes my chest feel warm, but it does. It's ridiculous. She's basically breaking and entering, and I'm over here finding it adorable.

The door clicks open, and we slip inside. The kitchen smells faintly of cinnamon and bird seed. On the counter, there's a half-empty bag of sunflower seeds. Hailey points to it like she's leading a nature documentary and turns around.

"Did you know sunflower seeds are a favorite for parrots, but too many can actually cause obesity? Their fat intake has to be carefully monitored," she whispers.

"Fascinating," I whisper back, though what I'm really fascinated with is the way her eyes light up when she shares these facts. It's like she's secretly delighted by someone's listening, even if we're really committing a crime.

We move into the living room, where the first cage sits by a window overlooking the street. A green parakeet tilts its head at us, feathers puffed like a tiny, feathered pom-pom. Hailey coos softly, sliding open the latch with practiced hands. There's a sign with stats in front of it with a price tag. She motions for me to hold the travel carrier open, and when the parakeet hops inside, she grins like we just pulled off a heist.

"One down," she says.

I nod, even though I'm mostly distracted by how the late afternoon sun slants through the lace curtains, making her eyes lighter. Or maybe I'm just a lovesick idiot. So much for casually seeing her. So much for not catching feelings.

We creep toward the next cage, and she adds quietly, "Pigeons can recognize themselves in mirrors, you know. Smarter than most people give them credit."

I bite back a laugh. "So you're saying if I buy a pigeon, it'll judge me?"

"It already is," she whispers, eyes twinkling.

"But that's not a pigeon," I whisper back.

"No, that's a conure." She holds the small parrot in her hands before adding him to the bag I'm holding. She continues until all four birds are secured in bags. She carries two outside, and I follow with the other two. The porch door closes behind us, and this time, instead of tiptoeing, she runs and opens the back door of the van, jumping in as soon as the bags are settled on the floor.

"Come on. Go, go go!" I do as I'm told, driving as fast I can without breaking the law. Somehow, rescuing birds in a small town in Florida feels like the most natural thing in the world. Everything else I've been worried about this past year fades into the background, because all that matters right now is making this girl happy.

SHE SMILES ear to ear on our way back to her place. Her head rests on the back of the seat, and with her eyes closed and her feet on the dashboard, she mumbles the lyrics to whatever song is playing. Something about a getaway car or something.

I don't speak so as not to disturb her from this peaceful, fulfilling moment. She looked so happy and so incredibly proud when we made it to the rescue center and they knew exactly what to do with the birds. She also called every pet store and sanctuary nearby to leave complaints about the lady. Most places didn't answer, considering it's nine PM on New Year's Eve, but she still left voice messages. I'm in awe of this woman, completely in awe.

We pull up to her house, and this time, she actually lets me open both doors for her—the van and the house. It's not much, but it makes me feel helpful, like my job here is being done.

Something I've learned about Hailey in these past few years is that the girl doesn't know how to ask for or accept help. The fact that she not only asked but also is letting me is a big deal. At least for me it is.

She plops herself on her cocoa couch, laying her head back and perching her shoeless feet on the arm rest. I take a seat by her feet, placing them on my lap.

"We're already late to the gala," I say.

She lets an exasperated breath out.

"Fuck the gala."

She surprises us both, but I don't even have time to ask anything, because she promptly continues, "I don't want to go. I don't want to get all dolled up to do the same thing I've done for the past decade. I already bought a ticket, or I guess you did, and my sister knows I support her. I just want to maybe enjoy a quiet New Year's Eve here."

Hailey lifts her head to look at me. "But I'm old and tired, and you're young and hot. You should go."

I clear my throat, shaking my head. "Do you think I flew all the way from Alaska so I could go to a gala just for the sake of going?"

"I mean, isn't that what you've done since we met? I figured the gala had some important meaning to you or something."

How is it that we've never talked about this? Oh yeah, I've never told her. Why would I when everyone around me just assumes whatever they want to assume and I just let them? It's a lot easier than the contrary.

She was so brave today, and that's admirable. People think I'm brave too because of what I do for a living, but really, it's not bravery. It's the feeling of being needed and wanted somewhere. It's the feeling that when they're about to lose hope, I'm the one bringing it back to them. But I can show some bravery now and just tell her.

"I crashed the gala the first time we met."

"What?" she asks, sitting up and giving me her full attention.

"I grew up near Atlanta and went to school with three guys: Travis, who you met briefly, Holt, and Axel. Axel moved to Amelia Island with his parents right after high school. Holt, Travis, and I were visiting him before starting bootcamp and decided it would be a good idea."

"Well, was it?" she asks, crossing her arms over her chest. "Not donating money to charity?"

I raise my hands in defeat. "We were three broke kids, okay?"

She huffs. "Well, continue."

"One thing led to another, and then the spill happened, and I met you. I couldn't get you out of my head, so Travis said he was in when I suggested we go back the following year. And now, well, now, it's the only time I get to see you."

She looks confused; maybe I just need to tell her with words.

"It was never about the gala, Hales." She sucks in a breath. "It was always about you."

She opens her mouth, but I don't let her utter a word. I want her to hear me loud and clear. I need her to know.

"If you were to tell me right now you'd like to meet in Hell every year, I would give you a list of sins I would commit just to make sure I was able to get in."

"Ash." I want to record the way she whispers my name so on long nights, I can listen to it on repeat. So on short days, it's the only sound I hear. So when I miss her, I can remember how lucky I am to have someone in my life who cares about me and the things I have to say enough to lose her voice in feelings. I'm undeserving, but I want to bottle it up.

"It's true."

"Are you sure you're twenty-three? Because I know older men who would never speak like that, let alone someone your age."

I pull her by her hand until she's sitting up straight, and I reach over to hold her face.

"What you don't understand is that age is just a number. It truly doesn't matter. My soul is aging with yours." She gasps when I pull her into my lap, my dick immediately coming to attention at the feel of her near me.

"I would also love for you to stop talking about other men in general, and I'll gladly make you forget there's anyone else out there but me." My hand traces her back until my fingers find the edge of her shirt and slide up, touching as much skin as I can. She's silent, not breathing. She's just looking at me in complete shock.

"And I'm almost twenty-four," I whisper against her lips before kissing her feverishly.

ALL OF THE **Stars by Ed Sheeran**

"DO YOU REALLY HAVE TO GO?" Hailey asks, her face buried in my chest. We spent three days together, completely tangled in each other, lost in the bubble we created.

We hiked, shopped, baked, and cooked together. We slept together, side by side, sharing a bed while we learned more about each other.

I like her. A lot. And judging by how she's acting, she likes me too.

"I—"

"I know it's unfair of me to even say anything at all, but I'm going to miss you, Ash," she interrupts.

"I'm going to miss you too. If you promise to still send me letters, I'll call." She peers at me through her dark eyelashes, and I can see her beautiful, glossy eyes. There are no tears, but they're full of an emotion that reaches deep within me.

"I'll write," she replies, twirling a piece of her hair between her fingers.

"Then I'll call." She eyes me with something I can't name, because what I think it is . . . it's definitely not what I want. I don't want to hurt her. That's the last thing I want to do, but there's nothing we can do when we live so far apart.

"Come here."

I open my arms again to her, and she takes the step to land in them. She fits perfectly, her head tucked against my chest, my chin resting above her head, her arms wrapped around me and mine holding her tight. We belong in this bubble of time where nothing else exists. Maybe, if I had something to give, we could make it work, but all I have is my job, and there's no station here. She has her family and friends here, all whom she loves. I can't ask her to move away. We're stuck in the in-between, and it sucks.

Time passes, quicker than I'd like, but it does. Another reminder this is not a dream, and real life awaits. She has to go be there for the kids in the hospital, and I have to go help keep people safe. I hope we find a way to heal from our own heartbreak or to let each other go if we can't. This is harder than I thought it would be.

"I have to go," I whisper against her soft hair. I take her in, letting the lemon and orange scent fill my lungs, allowing my fingers to commit to memory the way her hair feels between my fingers, the way her heart beats steadily in sync with mine. I take it all in one more time before kissing her head and taking a step back.

"I know." She drags her feet as she takes a step back and offers me a forced smile. "No complications, right?"

"If the stars align . . . " I let my words rest between us.

"And the seasons change," she echoes my words from last year.

"We'll see each other again," I complete the phrase. "Same time, same place."

She nods and starts walking back, unknowingly giving me the strength I need to take that plane back to where I belong.

"Goodbye, Asher. See you in twelve months!"

"Twelve months, Hales."

I wave shyly, waiting for her to turn and leave. *Please leave so I can do the right thing and get on my way too.*

She does eventually, and after her dark hair disappears through the glass doors at the Jacksonville airport, I go through security and head back to the place I now call home.

Dear Asher:

You know, there's something really interesting about having a relationship with someone nobody knows about. And by relationship, I mean friendship or whatever this is. Friends with benefits? The long-distance and sex once a year kind? Anyway, there's something really interesting about this—nobody really believes me when I tell them I have a friend they don't know who lives in a different state, all the way up there.

The interesting thing about it, beyond people not believing me, is that they all have opinions on why I talk about you so much or why I'd rather avoid discussing certain questions altogether. It's definitely interesting when they realize my sister's wedding is in two months and I have a plus one but no one to bring—then, they bring you up. I'm out of excuses, and really, I wouldn't forgive myself if I didn't ask, so this is me asking. Do you think you could take leave for a few days to go to this wedding with me? You totally don't have to, but I thought I'd ask.

Now that that's out of the way . . . I wanted to take a second to say thank you. I think this weekend with you was the best time I've had in a while. Thank you for helping with the birds and for going on so many little adventures with me. I feel refreshed, and it's been a long time since I did.

Apparently, my father wrote a letter to their neighbor about the birds and threatened to send the police next time. She moved, Asher, she moved! Hopefully, this is the end for her and the poor birds she's been neglecting.

I also wanted to say thank you for . . . I don't know, being here for me, I guess. I love that we've been able to grow this friendship with few expectations, knowing that at any point, we don't have to continue these yearly hang out thingies. As you know, the past few years have been tough, and knowing I can let go and be myself with you has been refreshing.

Now, tell me about you. Any interesting rescues lately? Let me know!

Xo,

Hales

Dear Hailey:

Happy Valentine's Day. This year, I'm early at least. I don't have a lot of time; life has been busy here, but I wanted to take the time and write back.

I'm glad I get to see you next month. I only have two days, so it won't be for long, but I'm glad either way.

How's work, Hales? I'm worried about you and your health. You can't keep going the way you have. It will kill you, even if not physically. You can die from the inside out—did you know that? I would hate for your beautiful light to be dimmed because of your job.

Let me know if there's anything I can do.

With warmth,

Ash

MAY, 2029

Dear Hailey:

Thank you for taking me to the wedding with you last month. I don't think I told you how much it meant to me, but it meant a whole lot. I loved getting to know your family and getting to see you around them. Last month was a dream, and being with you and yours was definitely something I've never seen before. Maybe part of it has to do with me not spending time with my friends' families growing up, because mine looked different, you know? But your family? The way they took me in like one of them, the way you all love each other? It's beautiful.

You are lucky to be loved by so many people, and I hope you don't take that for granted. But above all, they are lucky to be loved by you.

You have one of the most beautiful hearts I've ever known, and I hope you know how rare that is.

I know I brought up how concerned I am about you lately, but I'm serious. Would you do me a favor? Could you really consider your job? You need to do something for you, Hales. You need to take a step in the best direction for your health and happiness. I know you love it, but ask yourself what you love about it.

In the meantime . . . .how do you make holy water?

Think

About

It.

Think about it.

Okay.

You boil the hell out of it.

With love,

Asher

Dear Asher,

I did it. I put in for a transfer at work. I will be working in a different unit soon. I'm excited at the prospect of having some newfound balance in life and maybe finding a way to love nursing again.

I wish I only had good news to share, but I don't. My mom has been deteriorating so fast,

Ash, and I don't know what to do. It's breaking me, seeing her and my dad so sad. My siblings are all spiraling too, and I'm afraid I won't be strong enough to keep everyone together anymore.

Livie is struggling too. She and Alex are really going through it right now, and I don't know how to be there for her.

For the first time in a long time, I'm afraid, and I don't know what to do. My smile covering how much I'm crumbling inside is coming undone. Fast.

For the first time in a long time, I feel like I can't do it. I can't put on a brave face, I can't take care of everyone, and I don't know what to do.

It feels like I can't breathe, and for the first time in my life, I don't know how to fix it.

Do you have any advice? Or maybe more of those jokes?

Something.

Anything.

Xo,

Hales

Dear Hailey,

It breaks my heart reading how much you're hurting, how much your family and Livie are hurting. You are all good people; you don't deserve this, and I'm truly sorry.

At the risk of not giving you the happiness you need right now, let me share something with you. It breaks my heart to read your mom is sick and that you're all suffering. It means she was a present and involved mom at some point, and I can't say I ever had that.

My mom got pregnant at fifteen and my dad quit high school to provide for us. Nobody asked them to keep me or to bring me into a world in which I wasn't wanted, but that didn't stop them from letting me know every single day. My mom was miserable as a stay at home mom, but at least my dad didn't give up on the family, so she stayed and did her part. He, well, let's just say he hated me for stopping him from living his dream. Them living long and miserable lives while families like yours struggle isn't fair.

Here at sea, I see so much injustice. We almost lost a family recently, and we had to choose who to save first. We saved the kid *first and went back for the parents, and they almost didn't make it. While the three of them were in the water, it was obvious the mom wanted us to save the kid and the dad wanted us to save the mom. It was terrifying to see but also beautiful at the same time. Not one of them wanted to be rescued first. They were all putting each other first, and I've never seen anything like that until then. Actually, until I met you. Until I saw you around your family.*

Do you know why I love swimming so much? Other than being excellent at it? You can't hear screams underwater. It was the only place I could take space. The only place I could be myself. I could swim until my body gave out. And it felt great. The minute I found out I could help people doing it, I knew what I wanted out of life. I wanted to find a new one doing this.

You have so many people who depend on you, but who takes care of you? Who puts you first? Who wants you to be rescued first? I sure do, and I wish I could make you see that.

Make sure you remember that. You need to save yourself before you can save anyone else, even if it's hard.

With love,

Asher

SEPTEMBER, 2029

Dear Asher,

I've started this letter multiple times in the past two months. I'm so sorry I didn't reply sooner, but the struggle has been real.

I can't fathom a parent telling their child what yours did. You are so worthy of love. You don't have to get good grades or be the best at something in order to be loved.

It makes me so mad. So, so mad.

I have nothing positive to add to this conversation, and I have nothing positive to say about my life either, so I'm going to leave this here.

I did want to say you are deserving of love just because of who you are. You don't need to be the best at something or first in line or whatever it is they made you feel. Just by existing, everyone's worthy of love, you included. Actually, would it be weird for me to tell you I love you? I don't know how to explain it, but I do. I care about you so much, and all I think about is you and how easy it is to talk to you and share things with you, and I really, really, really wish we could be in the same place. I could show you how deserving of being loved you are.

Okay, before this gets weirder . . . Talk to you soon.

Xo,

Hales

Dear Asher:

I'm not going to apologize for telling you I love you, but maybe I'll apologize if it scared you. I didn't mean I wanted you to drop your whole life and move here. I didn't say it expecting something back, and after reading what you said about your parents, I fear that's how you took it.

I will apologize if it made you feel like that. It wasn't my intention. I just wanted you to know you are a very lovable person. I should have just waited, but my heart was in shambles after reading that, and I just needed to make you feel better.

That's all I do lately too—make sure everyone feels better. So if I made you feel bad, that's not what I wanted.

Would you write me back so I can stop spiraling and over-thinking?

That would be great.

Thanks.

Xo,

Hales

NOVEMBER, 2029

Dear Asher:

Not that you asked, but now, I'm mad. You haven't replied to any of my letters or read any of my texts. Are you alive? Are you okay? Short of flying to Alaska, I've tried everything. I just need you to tell me if you're okay.

Please just tell me you are.

Xo,

Hales

NOVEMBER, 2029

Dear Hailey:

I'm alive, but I'm not doing okay. I'll tell you more next month. Yeah?

Love,

Asher

5

NEW YEARS EVE 2029

when the party's over by Billie Eilish

HAILEY:

"SO, are you just going to sit here and look at the door all night?" Emma, my middle sister, says. She's sitting with her hands over her giant belly instead of dancing, because she's not trying to scramble the baby's brain. Those were her words, and I really just think it's adorable. She's carrying my niece in there, and she's taking really good care of her, even if she's already a little overbearing. She's worried about me, or so she says, and I feel a certain way about it. Everyone seems to be worrying about me lately, and I'm sick of it.

"What is the alternative, Emma?"

"Gee, I don't know. Date. Go out. Stop living in this fairytale you've formed in your head."

"Which one?"

"The one where you put your whole life on hold for a guy you get to see once a year at this gala. It's not healthy, babe," she replies.

I shake my head and look back to the door. He's not here. He said he was coming. He said he was going to talk to me, but he didn't even show.

Emma sighs. "It's almost midnight, Hailey. He's not coming," she deadpans.

I fight back the tears, tears I know will never stop falling if I let them out. All the emotions from the past couple of years will just come pouring out, and I can't risk it. Not here. Not now. If I'm going to break, it might as well be in private, where I can put myself back together again.

"I know," I whisper.

She squeezes my shoulders and lets out a breath. "I'm sorry."

My little empath of a sister, always so in tune with other people's emotions, but right now, there's nothing she can do to mend a heart she didn't break.

"Yeah, me too."

The countdown begins, and the shrimp drops while I stay with my hopes and dreams in this chair. My empty glass of wine balances in my hand as I look around and realize he not only stood me up, but he broke my heart in half too.

Dear Asher,

You know what's worse than waiting for you and you never coming? The fact that I miss sending these stupid letters. They became my diary, and I just blurted information out because I knew someone would read them and hopefully send one back.

Never a day in my life have I sent a letter. Never. And then you come along with your damn rules and your damn charm and all your winks and pretty smiles, and you turn my world upside down.

Well, congratulations, Asher. You did it. You turned it, and now you've left me in shambles.

I hope this letter pains you to read. I hope it brings you an ounce of the pain you've caused me on top of all the shit I've gone through. I hope it does.

Hailey

MAY, 2030

Dear Asher,

At this point, I don't even know why I bother writing to you. Habit, I guess. Annoyance too. Loneliness perhaps.

Life's gotten better, in case you were wondering. My mom stopped progressing. Well, her symptoms have. She's not the same as she was before, but she's not getting worse, and I'm taking that as a win. Finally, life has given me a win.

I'm having the hardest time doing anything outside of work. I got that transfer, so now I do more work, but it's less emotionally taxing. I read, I listen to music, and that's it. I sure as hell can't swim—it reminds me of you. I can't even go to Amelia Island without thinking about you. I can't do much without thinking about you, and it's fucking annoying.

I'm pathetic, I know. Maybe I just need to take your own advice and for once put myself first. I know I should cut you off, but for some bizarre reason, I can't.

Last letter, I told you I hope you were suffering but that's not the truth. The truth is, I really just hope you're happy. I really hope *you found someone else to love and that she makes you as happy as I couldn't.*

SEPTEMBER, 2030

Dear Asher,

I said I wasn't going to write to you again, yet here I am. My life is looking better, and I thought after sending you so many pouty letters, I figured I would send one with some good news.

First, I'm happier. I truly am. I finally found a balance with work, well kind of. I'm working only two shifts a week, which puts me at part-time, but I don't care. I like it a lot better. I started a side business, and my extra time goes to that. It's called Citrus & Oak. My mom and Emma help out sometimes. My mom, by the way, has not progressed again. She's staying where she's at, needing some help but still able to manage a lot. She still goes to therapy and to the doctor often, but it's not as much as before.

According to the doctors, this isn't typical, so we're thankful. Some of her medicine makes her sick, so she's been using some gummies, if you know what I mean, to help. She's been so funny and happy. We love it. It's given us our fun mom back. It's also made her really blunt, and she's been yelling at me for throwing my life away for many reasons—hence starting the side business.

Livie and Alex are talking about adoption; it has been really *good to see some hope in her eyes again. I can't wait to see them be parents. I don't think I'll be a mom. It's just not in the cards for me, and I'm older now. It's fine. I have beautiful nieces and nephews, and I can be a fun aunt. Maybe in another lifetime, I get the spouse, the baby, and everything else on my checklist. For this one, I'm happy with what I have, and I'm working toward staying that way.*

Now, the main reason I'm writing this is because I really need to stop acting like a 20 year old and get going with my life. I loved the years we spent together—or apart, I guess—and I'm thankful for everything you gave me, everything you shared with me, and I'm sure, one day, when I'm old, I'll tell all my nieces and nephews about the fling of a lifetime. In the meantime, keep saving people and living life large. So others may live, right?

I do hope you know that you deserve love. At the very least, I hope you find someone who can see how worthy of their love you are.

Goodbye, Asher.

Xo,
Hales

6

NEW YEARS EVE 2030

lovely by Billie Eilish and Khalid • PILLOWTALK by Zayn • Cold War by Cautious Clay • Someone You Loved by Lewis Capaldi • Breathe Again by Sara Bareilles

ASHER

HOW DOES one grovel when the fucking taxi won't hurry up? How does one show up ready to beg when there's a flight delay and now I'm running late? How do I tell her I was a fucking fool and that I love her too? How do I tell her it nearly killed me keeping her away, but that life was entirely too hard and she didn't need more on her plate?

Like that. You just tell her, Travis' words echo in my head.

"Here, here, here. Just drop me off." I can see the venue in the distance; I just need to get to her. Ten minutes to midnight, and I just need to see her.

It has to be this year.

It has to be now.

I open the door of the taxi and run down the busy street until I'm faced with the doors I've come to know like the back of my hand, the place that's felt like home for the past five years. I pray to a god I don't believe in that she's here and that she'll forgive me.

The room is, as usual, full of people dancing, spinning in circles and laughing. I search and search, skipping over everyone who isn't her—the blondes, the redheads, the men. I skip the height that is not quite right but still look in case her body has changed in the year and a half since I've seen her. I look for her friend, but I don't find lean legs, glossy brown hair, and pretty grey eyes. I don't find Hailey anywhere.

She didn't come.

Wow.

I walk the edge of the ballroom, seeking faces, but none are her. The music is boisterous, booming through the speakers and mimicking my heart.

Fast. Erratic. Loud. Obnoxious.

I should've just shown up at her house. I should've just come last year. I should've just kept my end of the deal.

She's not here.

I'm about to drop my efforts to find her, give up my last little bit of hope and walk away, when I see her. Wearing a beautiful silver dress with a deep v between her perfect breasts and sporting a smile I wish I was the reason for, Hailey stands in front of me.

She hasn't seen me yet, but I see her, dancing and smiling and . . . grinding her ass on a man. A man who has his hands all over her. *She found someone else.*

Of course she did. She's smart and funny and kind and beautiful. She loves her people wholeheartedly and she's a hard worker. Anyone would be lucky to be with her. I was just too dumb to see it.

Her eyes open for the first time, following the drop in tempo, and when she looks up, there are storm clouds in them when she meets mine. Hailey drops her hands to the side and immediately stops dancing. She looks just as torn as I feel, and I simultaneously love and hate it.

I step closer, moving so painfully slow, like my hands are in agony wanting to be near her.

Just like my heart and soul have felt for the past year and a half without seeing her, without talking to her.

This is exactly what I was afraid of: that my love for the sea and my love for Hailey would come to a crossroads where I had to pick. I picked the former while missing the latter. Missing her more than I thought possible.

Missing her more than I can bear.

Each step brings me closer to her, but she doesn't move. She doesn't do anything. She just stands there and blinks, as if she's trying to convince herself she really can see me.

Just before I reach her, she turns around, says something to the guy she was dancing with, and speedwalks out of the ballroom.

Are you here with him, Hales, or was this just a dance?

Did I already lose you without a chance to fight?

I follow her, like the man on a mission I am, but before she can slip away, I hold her arm. "Hales."

She pivots on her heels, snapping her eyes to mine—eyes filled with pure fury and anger. "Don't!"

"Don't what?" I ask.

"Show up here and look all happy to see me." Her tone is like nothing I've heard from her before. She's mad, rightfully so, but damn if it's not endearing to see sweet Hailey so worked up.

"I am, though. Happy to see you that is."

"Asher . . . it's been, what? A year and a half?"

"Eleven months since I last talked to you and twenty months since I last saw you," I add, trying to keep my voice from shaking.

I've been counting—has she? Do I have the right to ask? Probably not.

"A lot can change in twenty months," she says, and I nod.

"I know. I have." I have, but deep down, I'm just as in love with her as I was all those months ago. I just finally decided to set my fear aside and tell her.

I don't deserve her, I know that, but I will die trying. "But my feelings for you haven't," I continue. "My feelings for you are ever-growing while remaining grounded in one, simple truth."

Hailey throws her hands in the air and steps away from me, walking toward the bathroom that started it all. I let her but follow closely behind. I'm not missing the chance to speak to her. She doesn't make it to the bathroom, though; she stops, takes a deep breath, and turns around.

"You know what? No, I'm not going in there with you. I refuse to let you put me in the same spiral I was in for almost two damn years." She brings her hands to her hips. "I'm happy, Asher. Can you just be happy for me and let me be?"

"Are you, though? Truly happy?" I close the space between us and lower my voice so she not only hears it in her ears, but deep within her soul too.

"With who? Him?" I point the way we both came.

"I am." Her reply feels as shallow as a mud puddle. She's clearly lying, but is she lying to me or herself? Or both.

"Then why can't you look me in the eyes when you say that, huh?" She keeps her eyes on her feet because she knows—she knows I'll see the truth.

"Look at me, Hales." When she doesn't, I bring my fingers to her chin and lift her face up until her beautiful greys crash with mine.

"Tell me to leave," I command. "Tell me you don't want to know where I've been. Tell me we're done."

She doesn't say anything, but her eyes swell with tears. "Or, you can go back there and put an end to whatever that is and leave this place with me." I hold her gaze, reading the secrets they hide. I can see right through them, because my Hailey is still there, and I will relentlessly try to get her to forgive me.

"I—" she starts to say, but then she stops. She just stares. I look past her to the countdown. Two minutes.

Two minutes, and the place will be chaos.

Two minutes, and the spell breaks.

Two minutes, and everything can change again, just like it did five years ago.

But this decision cannot be mine. I fucked up, I know; it's up to her if I can be forgiven, but hell if I won't go down trying.

I step closer, taking in her citrus scent and the electricity coursing through my veins. "Lose him, Hailey," I whisper, my lips brushing the shell of her ear.

"I'll be out there." I point to the exit. "I'll wait for three minutes,

one past the shrimp drop. If you're not out there, it'll be the confirmation I need that our time has passed and what could've been will stay
like that."

"Ash." I bring my finger to her pretty, soft lips, stopping her.

"I read your letters." Surprise flashes through her eyes, as
ephemeral as this day has been. "I know I don't deserve your forgiveness, but I also know you told me I'm worthy of being loved."

I blink fast and hard. "Did you mean it?"

Her defensive head shake punctures my chest, but before I can say
anything, she closes her eyes tightly and nods. "Of course I meant it."
Her words are so soft and so quiet, I almost miss them.

"Then show me how. Please." I lift my hand to touch her velvet
skin, but I force myself away.

"Three minutes, Hales." I walk away from her, hoping I made the
right decision. Hoping whatever this is between us will last longer,
even if living in another state, across the country, will be a problem.

I sit and wait by the double doors, letting the breeze carrying the
scent of the ocean wrap me up while I feel hollow inside. The
crowd erupts into cheers inside, and I look at my watch. Happy
New Year and Happy Birthday to me. I let the true countdown
begin, the one that will let me know if I have to fly back to Alaska
with the other piece of my soul here or if I'll get to tell her how
much she means to me instead. 12:02, my watch reads, and I get my
answer. She's not coming. She's better off without me, as everyone
always is.

I get up, push off the wall, and walk toward the road. I hope I can
find a cab that will lead me back to where I came from. I should be
angry. At myself, at life, at the situation. At loving someone at the
wrong place and the wrong time.

I should be, but I'm not. Because meeting Hailey changed my life,
gave me something I never had before. It gave me meaning beyond
work. It gave me *life* again.

"Happy Birthday, Ash," Hailey's broken voice whispers from
behind me. It's loud enough for me to know it's her but low enough
that I can sense the fear behind it. I turn to find her out of breath,
standing by the wall where, just seconds ago, I was.

"Hales," I whisper back, and she runs until she leaps right into my arms.

She smells exactly the same. Like lemons and comfort. Like oranges and home. Her face is buried in my neck, and with muffled words, she says, "You have some explaining to do."

I wrap my arms tighter around her and nod. "I do."

"And groveling."

"I can do that," I reply, not dropping her from my arms. This hug feels like safe harbor from a storm. Being this close to her feels like the missing piece, and having her in my arms feels like coming home. *Home*, a word cursed before that now could mean everything I never knew to be possible.

"Thank you for giving me the chance to tell you." I put her down and hold her face, brushing her bangs away from her eyes and tracing her cheek with my thumb.

"Can we get out of here?" I ask, and she nods, getting her keys out of the small purse in her hands.

"But you drive, because I've been drinking."

I hold her hand and walk us through the parking lot, hitting the unlock button until I find her car. An SUV, not the van she drove last time I saw her.

"Nice ride."

"It was time. I'm not anywhere near the soccer mom I thought I would be by now, so why not?" She shrugs, taking the passenger seat.

"So where are we going?" I ask, hoping she says her hotel room or her house. Not so I can fuck her, but so we can have some privacy. I have a lot of explaining to do, and I don't want to be rushed.

"Not the hotel room," she replies.

I cock my head and raise an eyebrow at her. "Hailey, were you staying at the hotel with that man?"

She doesn't look at me, ignoring my question and not giving me the answer I wish she'd offered without hesitation.

"Did you fuck him?"

"You don't see me asking questions I don't want to know the answer to, Asher," she deadpans, delivering that blow exactly where she intended.

"What if I want to know?" I continue my drive down the quiet street.

"What if I don't want to tell you?"

"I thought I was your best friend." I look at her with a smirk, but she's not finding this amusing. Too soon?

"Well, then you disappeared, and now, here we are." Her exasperated breath could blow down a house. I need to back off. "Let's just go somewhere and talk." She lets out a breath.

I wait and see if she truly means it, but she does, and there's nothing I can do about it. Her eyes speak a language I'm not familiar with, and I hate that I need a translation.

"You told me to lose him and I did. Be happy about that and let's go. We can go to my house if that's easier." I nod, turning the car on and heading to Baker Oaks.

Her house looks and feels exactly the same, so then why does it feel like she's a completely different person? It feels like I don't know her anymore when deep down, I know I do. And I can't even blame anyone but myself on this one.

"Sit," she commands, taking her shoes off and leaving them in the middle of the living room. Who is this Hailey and what did she do with the Hailey from two years ago? I love seeing her like this, though, confident and sure of what she wants, even if it's my head right now.

She walks to the kitchen, and after cups clinking and cabinets doors closing, she appears back in the living room with a bottle of tequila.

"I'm not doing shots."

"Oh, this?" She holds the bottle up. "This is not for you. This is for me in case I need to clean my hands after I kill you." She sits across from me and crosses her legs. Her dress has a slit that goes all the way to her hip, and now, with her legs crossed, her thigh is exposed.

"Eyes up here, ocean cowboy." I do as she says and tilt my head to the side. The room is dim with only the lamp light, and she looks like an angel. My own angel.

"Ocean cowboy?" I ask.

"Always swimming toward danger and making all the girls lose their brain the minute you show up with your chocolate eyes, your sexy mustache, and those damn glasses. What happened to the contacts?" she asks with a wicked smile.

Oh, playful Hailey is here, and it's more nerve-wracking than angry Hailey. This Hailey was the one who gave zero fucks about consequences and kidnapped birds from someone's house.

"I needed to play every card I had up my sleeve."

"See, that's the problem, Asher. We played into this by pretending we live in a bubble. We're putting everything on hold for 364 days a year just to spend one day together." She sits forward, her elbows resting on her knees. "We got so intertwined with this fairytale bullshit, we forgot life was real, that real feelings were at stake here."

"I know. I don't think your feelings are a game," I add.

"You didn't show up."

"I know."

"You ghosted me. I thought something happened to you."

"I know."

"I sent letters. I texted. I called."

"I know, Hailey."

"Do you? Did you know how much I was hurting? You knew how hard everything was, and you still disappeared."

"I know."

"Stop saying you know! It's like your stupid *whats*. I know, I know, I know. What, what, what. Stop deflecting and just talk to me, Asher." The tears fall, the ones I was hoping she wasn't holding back. The ones that will tear me apart.

"I fucked up. I know. I have some reasons, but eventually, they ended up just being excuses."

"Go ahead. I'm listening." I open my mouth to start talking, but she says, "And please know, I'm judging."

I swallow hard and nod. The words I've been holding back for months feel like they're drowning me, each one heavier than the last.

"It's not easy to explain," I say, my voice quieter now. Can she tell this is hard for me too?

"You're right," I continue, rubbing my face, the stubble rough beneath my fingers. "I ghosted you, Hailey, and it was . . . it was because I was terrified."

"So was I, and you just left me out here alone."

"I'm sorry. I . . . I used to think I was cold and distant, but the reality is, I was protecting myself from feeling too much and not receiving it back." She opens her mouth to say something, but I raise my hand.

"Let me finish, please. Even if you don't like what I have to say."

Hailey nods and stays silent, allowing me to continue, "Not from you, but from everyone. With you, though, I *felt* too much. And the more I felt, the more I pulled away. Does that make sense?" The way she's looking at me tells me the complete opposite. Her eyes have lost all the warmth, replaced with icy cold stones. They're like galena— absolutely gorgeous, but also deadly.

Her eyes narrow, but I continue. "I lost someone." A loud breath leaves my mouth, ripping right through my soul. "A girl. Young and full of life. She was kayaking with her dad, and they got caught in a cave. She hit her head and broke her leg." I close my eyes, trying to forget.

"It was like any other rescue, but when I got into the cave, I couldn't breathe. She looked just like you. I couldn't breathe. I couldn't think. It felt like déjà vu, but not the good kind. It was like I was drowning in something familiar, and I thought . . . I thought it was the same thing you were feeling but miles and miles away, by yourself."

I pause, the silence thick between us. It's hard to say the rest, to admit the real fear that kept me away.

"The thing is, I care too much. I care more than I know how to handle. And I was so damn scared of loving you and not being enough for you, Hailey. I was terrified I'd screw it all up. It felt like the universe was giving me a second chance, but I didn't know if I could actually handle it. I thought if I just stayed away, didn't make any promises, didn't let you get close enough to see the mess I am . . . maybe I wouldn't ruin it like I ruined everything else. Because even though I held her, even though I swam back with tears in my eyes because it felt like I had you in my arms, she didn't make it."

The words are coming faster now, like I can't stop them, like they've been stuck inside me for too long and I'm spilling out every-thing I never said.

"I know that sounds like the dumbest shit, but that's the truth. I didn't just disappear because I didn't care. I disappeared because I cared too much. I pushed you away before I could prove I wasn't good enough for you. And I live there and you live here; I can't ask you to leave your home and I can't leave mine. Not yet, at least." I wipe away a tear roaming free.

"And every day I spent away from you, every day I convinced myself this was easier, was worse than the day before. Because at least when I had you, I had the illusion that maybe, just maybe, I wasn't going to screw this up. But I was too scared to even try." I let out a broken sob and notice Hailey is crying too.

"I'm broken, and I live far away, and even the one thing I'm good at, I still fuck up sometimes and lives are lost. You deserve better, Hales, but I couldn't live with myself anymore if I didn't tell you all of this."

The silence that follows feels like a punishment, but I need it. I need her to understand, to see me as something other than a selfish idiot who runs away when things get too real.

"I didn't want you to think you did anything wrong, because you didn't. You are perfect and I miss you. I don't know how this would work, but I need you in my life again. If you'll have me."

She stands, wiping away tears from her cheeks and making my heart thump in my chest louder and faster. She sits on my lap and rakes her hands through my hair, all the way down to my neck. I wipe the tear from her lip before kissing it gently. "I'm sorry. I truly am. I didn't mean to hurt you."

"But you did," she whispers.

"I know."

"This is the definition of insanity, you know?" Her fingers inter-twine behind my neck, a sad smile on her face.

"What is?"

"Doing the same thing and expecting a different outcome."

"Then call me insane, baby." She closes her mouth over mine, kissing me gently at first but shifting the intensity before I realize she's kissing me as though this is the last time she'll taste my lips.

"Wait," I whisper. I must be losing my mind, because this is exactly what I wanted to happen, but I need to make sure she's okay.

She lets out a breathy whimper, disappointed about my sudden interruption. "Ash, we can talk more later, but I missed you. I get it—you were trying to protect me or whatever. You were in a bad space, I get it." She tunnels her fingers through my hair, cradling my head to her chest. "I get it, but right now, I need to know if your body missed mine as much as I missed yours. I need you to remind me how good we are for each other."

She pulls my head back, her pretty eyes locked on mine. The peace and the understanding I find in hers are undeserving, but I'm greedy and I'll take it anyway.

"We can figure out the rest in the morning."

Her lips touch mine, tentative and kind, showing me forgiveness with every stroke of her tongue on my lips, with every moan and whimper she lets out as our tongues dance.

"For now, show me, Asher." Her words are a pant of want and need. "Show me how much you missed me." My lips crash onto hers, desperate to taste, desperate to explore, to remember. I need to remind my brain why we're good together—why we belong together. My heart already knows; it's time for my brain to catch up.

She tastes fresh. She's like the sweetest morsel of your favorite dessert after you've been restraining yourself.

She's like the first breath of fresh air after being underwater for too long. I've been drowning in the thought of her, and now, I finally have her in my arms again. I'm ready to breathe again.

She straddles me as she tilts her head back and exposes her neck, inviting me to kiss and suck the tender flesh the way we both love. She moans the second my teeth bite into her neck.

I stand, Hailey's legs wrapping around me and her soft whimpers filling the space. I kiss and tease. I bite and lick—all the way to her bedroom.

The lights are off, and clumsily, we make it through to the bed. There's nothing to trip over because, as usual, there's no mess. Always so put together and tidy, but she loves her sex messy and rough. My sweet contradiction, one I know so well.

I pull her dress down her arms, and it falls swiftly to the floor, leaving her in nothing but thin lace underwear. I graze her skin of her back, my knuckles leaving goosebumps in their wake until I reach bare ass. A thong, just like I knew she would be wearing.

I take my time touching her body, tracing every inch of skin available for me to touch, kissing her mouth, licking her chin, and biting her collarbone. I lower her to the bed, laying her on her back and bending her leg as I kiss her breast.

"Ash," she cries out when I bite her nipple and push her panties to the side.

I bite harder, and she sucks in a breath, followed by a moan. I want to make her forget the almost two years we were apart. I want to make her forget all the bad things and just remember how good we are together.

I want to remember it too.

"There's two of those, you know," she snarks, and I smile against her nipple, moving to the other one and giving it the attention she wants.

With her nipple in my mouth and her wet pussy under my thumb, I tease and touch until she's gasping asking for more. I want to give her everything she wants, but first . . . "I need you to come." She's wet and soft and perfect. Her clit hardens under my thumb as her back arches against me.

"You're so perfect." My words tip her over the edge as she snaps her legs closed and unravels under my touch. I kiss her through her orgasm, climbing up her body, kissing through the valley between her breasts to her neck and her lips.

"Fuck me, Asher, please."

God, I love it when she asks for what she wants.

"I love it when you ask so nicely, baby."

"I'm not asking, I'm begging. Please," she pleads, and who am I to deny her? I pull my pants down, discarding my clothes in the pile we left behind. I do the same with her thong, but before I do anything else, I look at her—laying on her bed, her pretty hair cascading around her, her flushed cheeks. She's stunning, and she's all mine—at least for tonight.

"Is that?" she asks, eyes trained on my thigh, right on the tattoo that once upon a time was only a rock surrounded by waves—now, it's complete.

"A lighthouse," I whisper, rendering her speechless. A small light-house sitting at the top of the rock, with an H as the lightbulb. "I told you. My beacon of light, *you*."

She gasps, emotion filling her eyes, but I want to do more than just let her see the little tattoo I got in her honor. I needed her permanently imprinted on my skin, just like she is in my heart too.

My hands explore her body, from her toes, up her thighs, caressing her hips and caging her in.

"You're perfect," I whisper against her lips, aligning my dick with her entrance. I tease and tease but don't enter her, and she lets out a grunt.

"You already said that. Now, fuck me. *Please*."

What I wouldn't give this woman. I thrust into her hard, feeling her walls tighten around me immediately. Her lips part when a gasp escapes her, and I all but whimper. She's soft and wet and warm. She closes her eyes as she takes it all. As she feels it all. Her back arches and her hands grip my hair, pulling it gently, pulling me to her. I'm letting her know with my body what I feel for her. How I feel about her. In this moment, she's all I need.

"Fuck," she moans as I hit the spot I know makes her feel good.

"Tell me, Hales. Did he make you feel like this?" I want to take away all the bad feelings I may have caused and give her only plea-sure. I want to show her there's only me.

She doesn't say anything, and I pinch her nipple. She gasps. "Answer me, Hales. Did he make you feel this good?" I hit the spot again, and this time, her eyes open wide before she shakes her head.

I nod knowingly. "It's because you are mine and I'm yours." I pinch her nipple again, and her mouth opens on a plea.

"More," she groans, her fingers crawling down my arms and holding my hand, guiding it to her neck. My eyes open wide, and she smiles. "I said more."

I squeeze my fingers gently, feeling her heartbeat under my fingertips and seeing if this is what she wants. I'm so lost in her, I just . . . "Fuck, Hales." My words carry everything I feel right now that I cannot eloquently say in any other way.

Hailey arches her back, pushing her breast against me as her glossy grey eyes darken to stormy grey. Her gaze alone could tip me over the edge, but it's her inner walls squeezing my dick that does it. She closes her eyes and opens her mouth on a silent plea, her legs shaking, her nails scratching, her breathing racing. I'm done for, completely gone for her, finally closing the space we put between us, beyond the distance.

OCEAN EYES by Billie Eilish

LONG, soft hair covers my chest as little snores vibrate through the space.

How am I going to make this work?

I know I have to, especially considering how shitty this past year and half has been. I thought keeping her at bay was what was needed for both of us, but clearly, this is where we belong—intertwined in bed, her legs draped over mine and our hearts beating in sync. Her soft snores even out, stopping all together as she tries to move from my hold. I keep my arm wrapped around her, holding her in place.

"Good morning, sleepy head," I whisper, kissing the top of her head.

She groans and stirs. "Happy Birthday, Ash." Her ocean eyes meet mine, stealing my breath and putting everything into perspective once again. No matter what, we need to make this work.

"Thank you, beautiful."

"Oh, please. I probably look like I've been hit by a truck." She stretches her arms, making noises that should not hit me all the way in my groin, but they do. I grunt.

"Someone's not a morning person," she comments, sliding her hand down to my dick. "But something else *is.*"

Her devilish smile makes me want to do whatever it is she's thinking, but we can't because— "We need to talk."

"You're no fun." Hailey pouts. If I didn't know better, I would say she's deflecting, but the Hailey who was pissed last night is not the Hailey in my arms right now, and I don't understand the switch.

I sit up, sliding my glasses on and covering my hard on with a pillow. Of course it won't go down when I have this girl near me. Her scent, her taste on my lips from last night, and just the sight of her would do it, let alone her sitting right there naked.

"How do you expect me to have a conversation with you when you look like that after you just woke up?" she adds, roaming her finger in the air around my body.

I let out a sigh, because somehow, we're so in sync, she feels the same way I do. "Because we're adults, Hailey, and we can put our lust and desire aside for a minute so we can talk, yeah?"

She rolls her eyes. "Sure. Do you want coffee?"

I nod, and in an instant, she parades her naked body out of the room and leaves me alone with my thoughts. What is the conversation I'm actually going to have here? Yes, I want to date her, but I need to figure out what that looks like for us, with her here and me there.

Hailey comes back while I'm lost in thought, wearing an oversized t-shirt, two cups of coffee in hand. "I could have made the coffee," I say, and she smiles softly at me.

"I wanted to do it." She's such a caregiver, even in the simple things like making coffee in the morning. She sits across from me, a leg under her and coffee in both hands.

"Tell me, Asher Hunter: what do we need to talk about?"

"Us," I mutter.

"There isn't an us, though, right?" She takes a sip and winces, either from the temperature of her drink or the words coming out of her mouth. "I mean, there isn't anything between us beyond fucking once a year on New Year's Eve—or am I mistaken?"

"Hales," I whisper.

"Am I wrong?"

I shake my head and bite my lip, considering her words. Then, it hits me: she is wrong. "You said you loved me."

"And that was clearly a mistake, because—"

"No," I interrupt. "You don't get to call loving me a mistake. Not when nobody has ever loved me a day in my life, and you so freely gave me your love. Unless you truly mean it, and what you felt was euphoria and excitement, not really love."

She lets out a sigh, but there's not a tear in sight. I'm so used to watching movies where the first thing women do when they're upset is cry that I'm conditioned to expect it, but shit, that's wrong. So wrong. This calm façade she's sporting gives me more information than almost any word can.

She finally shakes her head.

"No, what? No, you don't love me, or no, I'm not a mistake?"

"You're not a mistake, Asher." She takes another sip of her coffee. "And I do love you." The storm brewing in her eyes breaks through, and she's finally showing everything she's been hiding. I see it as clear as day: fear. She's afraid of loving me. That, I can work with.

Setting the coffee on the nightstand, I reach forward and hold her face. "Good, because I happen to love you too."

She gasps.

"I'm pretty sure I fell in love with you before I knew your name, Hales. Back when you were my mystery girl." My face softens into a smile. "The mere idea of you was love-worthy, and the real thing has been even better."

I try to show with more than my words how much I mean it. I hope she not only hears it but feels it too. "I told you I dreamed of you five years ago, but the reality of being with you can't compare. This is so much better."

"But you didn't come back."

"I know. I told you why. I was going through hell." It's true. I'm sorry, and I hope she knows I mean both truly.

"Why didn't you tell me?" she asks, panic behind her eyes.

Caregiver, first and foremost. Oh, my Hales, but who takes care of you? "You have a lot on your plate, and I didn't want to add more to it."

"And you thought disappearing for months and then just showing up here is any better? I thought you died, Ash!" She gets up and paces the room. "I set up a Google alert for your name and called your station. Nobody said anything; they just said they were not allowed to disclose any information. And you were hurting this whole time?"

I walk to her, holding her face with both hands, daring her to keep her eyes on mine and see the truth in them. "I was hurting. I didn't know how to handle it, and all I kept thinking about was your mom needing you here. I eventually was fine. Do you hear me?"

I take her face in my hands, and hold her gaze. "I'm not hurting anymore. You don't have to take care of me."

"Did you ever stop to think that maybe I wanted to take care of you, you freaking—"

"If you say ocean cowboy, baby, I'm going to laugh."

She narrows her eyes. "If you say ocean cowboy, baby," she mocks, rolling her eyes. She's going to give herself whiplash if she doesn't keep them in check.

"You called me baby."

"No, you did. I was just repeating," she quips.

"I want to be *your* baby." My words are playful now, trying to ease the tension.

"And I want to cure cancer but there are things we can't have."

She takes a step back, releasing her face from my hold and turning around. To what? Leave this conversation? No, ma'am.

"Tell me you don't want me."

She freezes.

"Tell me sending me monthly letters and seeing me once a year is enough."

She stands there, back to me, clenching her fists.

"Tell me it's enough, and I'll find a way for it to be enough for me too, because I'd rather have you once a year than not at all."

She shakes her head.

"But if not, let's make this work. Let's make *us* work." She turns around, finally. Her cheeks are red, her eyes are glossy, and her lip is bleeding from her biting it. I raise my hand, dip my finger behind her lip, and free it from her teeth.

"What do you say?"

She nods.

"I need more than that, baby. I need you to be sure."

"If you don't stop calling me baby, I'm going to cry, and I'm trying hard not to." I can see her holding back tears, clear as day.

I step forward. "Why?"

"Asher Hunter, did you learn a new question?"

"For fuck's sake, woman."

We both shake our heads. She giggles, and a tear falls free. "There it is."

I bring her into my arms. "Let yourself cry. I've got you."

She breaks into small sobs while whispering incoherent thoughts that sound a lot like *I love you* and *we will figure this out.*

I really hope we do.

FEBRUARY, 2031

Dear Hailey,

I'm writing this after we just hung up the phone, but I told you I love letters, so I'm going to keep sending them. I told you we would make this work, and I'm trying, baby. I hope you see that. You told me you were afraid of jumping into a long distance relationship but that you were going to be brave and give us a try. I acted all nonchalant like I'm a fearless asshole. It's a lot easier to write my feelings than say them out loud, so I'm here writing all the things I'm afraid to tell you.

I'm afraid to tell you how many fears I have because you think I'm a fearless water cowboy and I have to live up to my name.

I'm afraid this is all a dream, that I'm going to wake up any time now and you either don't exist or you will leave me.

I'm afraid to move away from Alaska and leave the one thing I'm good at, but I'm also afraid of asking you to move here and having you hate it because you miss everyone.

I'm afraid you'll move here either way because that's who you are as a person. I'm afraid you'll hate me for it.

I'm afraid I'll die at sea and leave you alone.

I'm afraid I'll quit my job so I don't die at sea, be miserable the rest of my life, and eventually leave you alone anyway.

I'm afraid of loving you the way I do and you breaking my heart.

I'm afraid of not knowing how to love you right because I've never been loved. Not the way I know you deserve to be loved, at least.

I'm not afraid of jumping from a helicopter or swimming for hours in frigid waters, but I'm terrified of hurting you. I hope you know that.

With all my love,

Ash

MARCH, , 2031

Dear Asher:

So we were on the phone and I got your letter. I shoved it in the nightstand because you were telling me very naughty things you wanted to do to me. I've been a horny mess for weeks, so a girl's gotta do what a girl's gotta do, right?

Anyway, sorry this is weeks later, but I wanted you to know I read it and I love you more for it.

Thank you for opening up to me. I can't imagine how hard it is for you to say all these things when you grew up making yourself small and without space to be yourself. Nobody should grow up like that. And this is me telling you, I am your safe space. I'm about to love you so hard, there won't be a doubt in your mind how worthy of love you are.

Fear is not a bad thing. It means you care so much about something, your body is triggering a survival response. Fear is that response. But, my love, we can change that for hope.

We can hope you don't die at sea.

We can hope we last forever.

We can hope wherever we end up living will make us both happy.

I know I'm real and I know this is real, so no need to fear that. And you don't need to fear not loving me right, because you already do.

I love you, Asher Hunter, with everything I have. We will figure things out.

In the meantime, phone sex is working out great.

Xo,
Hales

7

APRIL, 2031

I Will Wait by Mumford & Sons
&
Collide by Howie Day

HAILEY

ME:

Asher, answer the phone.

ME:

Ash

ME:

I'm okay. Don't freak out, but I need you to call me back.

ME:

It's been 24 hours, and I swear, Asher Hunter, if you don't add me to your damn emergency contact list so Lisa can tell me if you're alive . . .

ME:

that's it, I'm taking a damn plane to Alaska.

I toss my phone onto my bed and scream. Is screaming even a thing if nobody else can hear it? I mean, I can, so that means it is, right? What in the actual fuck am I going to do? And why am I talking to myself? I'm losing my mind.

Losing my mind.

Why is he not answering the damn phone?

All I want to do is call Livie, but how do you tell your best friend who has been trying for years to conceive that you accidentally got pregnant. Who gets pregnant this easy at thirty seven after fucking a man once? Well, we did fuck like eight times that weekend, but like, what the hell?

I can't tell my mom—she'll have so many questions. Same with all my siblings. And the one person I want to talk to about it is out there rescuing who knows who and not fucking answering the phone.

The spiral might have conjured him into existence, because my phone is ringing.

On the bed.

Where I tossed it.

On the other side of the room.

It's like I'm twelve again and the boy I have a crush on is about to find out. I mean, I don't expect him to do anything, since I decided I'm keeping the baby regardless of what he says, so I'll have to deal with my own decisions.

And . . . he hung up the phone. Damn it, Hailey.

I grab the phone and call him back.

"I'm sorry, I was on a mission and my phone was at my place. What's wrong?" he says after not letting the phone ring once.

I let out a breath. *So he is alive.*

"Baby?"

I laugh.

Yup, that's exactly it.

A baby is all I want to say. "I'm fine."

"Hailey." His annoyance is clear. "I thought we talked about this. I thought something happened to you or your mom."

"I know," I whisper, but he continues.

"My brain has been hardwired to worst case scenario, and all the texts—"

"I know," I interrupt. "I'm sorry."

"I've had thirty six hours of hell. Can I call you back after I shower and sleep if you're fine?"

"No."

"No what?"

"No, we need to talk now, but I need you to video call me."

"I look like shit."

Like he could ever. I'm going to chicken out and not say anything, but he needs to know, right? So I need to look at him when I tell him. I need to know what his thoughts are about this. He deserves to know.

I click accept on the request to video chat, and damn, he was right. He looks rough.

"I told you." His eyes shine with elation and humor. Damn it— even now, he's making *me* laugh.

"No, no, you look great."

"Now don't be lying to me. It's fine. You just have never seen this side of me. I'm still sexy and I know it."

He did not go there. I scoff.

"So now that you're not tense and shit, what is it you wanted to tell me?" He lies back in a chair, his arm flexing behind his head highlighting his damn sexy veins, and I'm drooling. He closes his glassses framed eyes and smacks his lips. I've never in my life wanted to crawl through the phone before.

"I'm pregnant!" I blurt out before I can stop myself from changing this man's life forever. I have no clue if he wants kids. We're not even *together* together, I don't think. Oh fuck, we don't even live in the same area. Damn it, why didn't I think this through? *Well, Hailey, you didn't have to think anything through, because you didn't plan for this.*

"Hailey!" he shouts, snapping me from my thoughts.

"What?" I shout back.

"What did you just say?"

"What?"

"What? What?"

"Oh, dear God, here we go again."

I'm deflecting now. Can he tell? Can he tell I might lose it if he's not happy about this? Or worse—if he isn't but tells me he is just to spend years and years resenting me? I can't do this.

"Hailey!" What? This time, I shout it in my head. Breathe and focus. Breathe and focus. "Please, you're not making any sense." He's concerned, and I don't blame him.

"Whatever it is, just tell me. I think I heard you, but I want to be sure." His posture changes, from laid back and relaxed to attentive and worried. Damn it. I don't want him to worry.

I sit and prop my phone on the table, taking a deep breath. "I'm pregnant, Asher."

He nods patiently. "That's what I thought you said. How are you feeling about it?"

He's so calm, as if I didn't just tell him I'm having a baby. An unplanned baby. *His baby.*

"What do you mean?"

"I mean . . . " He pauses and crosses his legs. "I want to know what you're thinking about this pregnancy."

"Why?"

"Well, because it's your body carrying an embryo right now, and I'm not a woman, so I have zero clue how this is affecting you. I know you want kids, but that's about as far as we've talked about it, you know?"

I nod. "It's not an embryo anymore."

His eyes widen. Why is he in shock? It's fucking April. I'm seventeen weeks pregnant.

Oh shit.

"Asher, it's your baby." His eyes water, clear as day. "I'm pregnant with *your* baby." He doesn't say anything; he just nods.

"I didn't want to ask."

This man. He was just cool, calm, collected, even if the baby wasn't his?

"Do you think I've been fucking someone else?"

He shrugs. "You told me not to ask questions I didn't want to know the answer to, and I definitely didn't want to know the answer to that."

This very much infuriating man will be the death of me. Death by orgasm. Death by calmness. Death by stupid shit he says.

"We literally said four months ago we would be in a relationship. Have *you* been fucking someone else?"

Unbelievable.

"I haven't slept with anyone else in five years, Hales. Just you."

What? There's no way. No way. "Yeah right." I roll my eyes.

"I kissed this girl once, and she's kind of occupied my whole mind since." He smiles softly. "I haven't been able to think or look at anybody else." He reclines again, legs crossed, arm behind his head, pretty smile. "I'm not complaining about it either."

How does he expect me to survive him? To get over him? To just accept he, what? Met me once and has never been able to get me out of his head like this is a romance movie?

"My question still stands, though. How are you feeling about it?" he asks.

Scared. Angry. Excited. But I can't say any of that.

"Don't lie to me, baby. I can see you trying to figure out what you think I want to hear when what I really want to hear is how *you* feel about it."

I let out a breath from deep within me. I don't think I've ever been asked to honestly say how I'm feeling, and that alone is going to make me lose my carefully crafted control.

"Excited?" It comes out as a question.

"Scared," I add, covering my face with my hands.

"I can see how those two emotions mingle. What do you want from me right now?"

That's it. I can't fucking do it. "Asher, I swear on my heart, if you don't start showing me some damn emotion, I'm going to lose my shit!"

"I'm trying really hard *not* to show you any emotion, because ultimately, it's your decision. I don't want you to take *me* into consideration."

"Why?"

He shows me a kindness that nobody has ever shown me, and it's nerve-wracking. "Because you're so selfless, you will do whatever you think you *should* do as opposed to whatever you *want* to do."

I consider him and his words. I've thought about everything but this. I've thought about what would be best for everyone, not myself. But in an instant, I have no questions in my mind about it. I want this baby. I want this baby with *him*. Because this? This is not what I expected from him, but I should've known better. "I want this baby."

He nods.

"But you don't have to want it. I'm completely—"

"I want this baby too."

"Like I've made up my mind, and I can do it—"

"I want this baby too, Hales."

"And if you want to you can be a part of—"

"Hailey!" he shouts, startling me. When my eyes meet his, he smiles. "I need you to stop spiraling for a second and hear me out."

I open my mouth but decide against saying anything. "I stopped. Go ahead."

"I want this baby too."

He wants this baby?

"But you live in Alaska."

He lives in Alaska? Hailey, what are you, twelve?

"We can figure out logistics as we go, but I want this baby too. I want to have this baby *with* you."

I let out a broken sob. The one I was too afraid to let out. The one I've been holding deep inside my soul for years. "Good, because I think I want this baby with you too."

He yawns, and guilt hits me tenfold. "Thank you," he whispers groggily.

"For what? For getting pregnant on accident and complicating our lives even more?" I wipe away a tear.

"For making me feel whole again." He smiles, and it reaches his tired eyes.

"I love you, but you should go to sleep. Just call me when you wake up, okay?" Crisis averted—for right now, at least. He needs to sleep so he can make sure this is actually what he wants before we talk things through.

"I'm not going to change my mind." How does he know? What the hell? "When I wake up, we're going to talk about this, but I'm not changing my mind. I want you both."

My throat releases a sound I can't name. A cough? A giggle? A gargle? Something, but whatever it is, it's relief. Relief that he sees me. Relief that he understands. Relief that I might actually be okay.

"Okay."

"Okay. Give me twelve hours, and I'll call you back." I nod. "I love you, Hales."

"Love you too."

"Now, hang up," he commands.

I roll my eyes. This little game he's been playing of not wanting to be the one to say goodbye or hang up the phone first has been going on for months. "Not this again."

"Hang up, baby. I need to sleep, and I can't be the one to do it." I roll my eyes. This man wants to make my heart race one way or another. "Have some mercy on me."

I'll take happily annoyed any day. "Fine. Bye, Asher."

"Bye, Hales." I hang up the phone and toss myself on to the couch. I guess we're doing this.

We're having a baby.

8

JULY 3031

I GUESS I'M IN LOVE by Clinton Kane • Wildfire by Cautious Clay • A Thousand Years by James Arthur

ASHER

I FINISH SEASONING the burgers right as there's a knock on the door. "Hold on!" I wash my hands quickly. I told these motherfuckers not to come until later, but they don't listen to any command ever, including when to show up for dinner.

"What happ—" The words die in my throat, because on the other side of the door is a wish come true. I rub my eyes to make sure I'm not seeing the wrong thing, that it's reality and not a dream.

"Well, are you going to let my giant ass in, or are you going to stand there with your jaw on the floor?" Hailey says, holding multiple bags with a smile. She's so beautiful—she always is, but standing in front of me, outside my door while carrying our baby, she's breathtaking.

I pick her up, holding her close. She fits perfectly, belly and all. "Put me down!" she shouts, and I smile with a mouthful of her hair.

"You're here." My words whisper the longing I've felt deep in my soul. Is this reality? She didn't mention this at all, and we talked, what? A few days ago? I have so many questions. I put her down, kissing her softly before I lead her inside, carrying her bags with me.

I help her sit and pull her shoes off. She must be tired. It's not easy to get here. *How* did she get here?

"I'm pregnant, not incapable, Ash." She laughs. Her laugh . . . I've missed it. I've wanted to hear it live, near me. I've wanted to be in the same place where her laugh is. I've wanted to be the one to make her laugh.

"Let me." I look at her, waiting for permission, one she doesn't grant. "Please." She nods and I slide her socks off too.

I sit across from her, quietly massaging her feet while she sinks deeper into the couch. We talked about seeing each other soon. I requested leave, but shit kept happening here. It's not as easy as just taking off and showing up somewhere when you live in the middle of nowhere, but I guess where there's a will, there's a way, because she *is* here.

"What are you doing here?"

"I wanted to see you," she replies.

My heart. My whole heart.

"I wanted to see you too, but this is so far." Far is an understatement. She either flew here from Anchorage, or she took the almost ten hour ferry. Or a float plane. All of those are inconvenient. At least it's summer and not stupid cold right now.

"It is, but I had nowhere else to be." She shrugs nonchalantly.

"I thought your family hosts a Fourth of July party or something." I switch feet, grabbing and massaging the other. She moves her bangs out of the way, but they return to their stubborn spot. It's a habit she has that I love. The hair won't stay off her face, but she does it anyway.

She closes her eyes and smacks her tongue. "Yeah, well, I've participated in those for almost thirty-seven years, but I've never spent a holiday weekend with the father of my child, so coming seemed like a good idea." I kiss her foot, and she startles. "Ew, don't do that."

My laugh bounces off the walls and fills the space. "Not a foot person?"

"No, and I didn't think you were either."

I shake my head. "I'm a *you* person."

I smile, taking it all in: her in here in my space, in my house, in my quiet room. Suddenly, the entire place is filled with color and meaning. All because she's here. She's my whole world, how have I not seen this before?

"How long are you here for?" I ask—the question I really want to know the answer to. I want to know if I should cancel the dinner tonight and get lost in her for hours.

I need to know if I need to call work and tell them nobody better need me for the next forty-eight hours.

I want to know.

I *need* to know.

She rises to her elbows and loses the playfulness she's been sporting since she got here. "A month—if you'll have me."

"Don't play with my feelings, because you know if it were up to me, I'd want you here forever." I mean every word.

She waves. "Forever sounds good."

What does she mean by that? "What?" I'm destined to be confused by this woman forever, I guess.

"Living with you forever and not doing this once a year bullshit we thought was a good idea sounds better than anything, to be honest." She pauses, and I hope she's not lying. I really hope she means it.

I'll put a ring on her finger right now if that's true.

"You said you were afraid of asking me to move here, so you don't have to. I'm here if you want me . . . but I figured a month would be a good time for us to figure our shit out." She lays her head back down and closes her pretty eyes, her eyelashes kissing her cheeks. "I also think your son would love to kick his daddy too, not just me."

My son?

She's having a boy?

We're having a boy?

What is happening?

"We're having a boy?" I ask, my voice breaking.

She nods, and all the air leaves my body. I can't find words to convey what I'm feeling right now, so I don't say anything. I just sit and look at her.

She's so beautiful. She always has been, but her carrying my child has to be the best view. Not clear, pristine waters or the highest peaks, not moss covered trees or the dramatic coastlines I see every day. Not salmon in streams or majestic bears. Not glaciers or midnight sun. None of them compare to her flawless beauty.

"Let me see," I whisper.

Gray eyes meet mine, and with a wicked smile, she lifts her white shirt, revealing the most perfect bump I've ever seen. She shows me when we video chat and I've seen pictures, but nothing compares to seeing it right now. She's so beautiful. So perfect. And she's here.

"Permission to touch," I whisper, echoing the words she said all those years ago when I was afraid of her touch, when I didn't know someone else touching you could be because they wanted to make you feel good, not because they wanted to harm or use you. Back when I didn't know life could have this precious meaning.

She nods, and I slide my hands up her leggings, lowering the band over her belly, finally seeing it all in its glory. Round, with a dark line in the middle leading to my favorite place on Earth.

Perfect, just like all of her.

My hands immediately gravitate toward it, as if I was metal and she and that baby are the strongest magnet.

But it's not enough.

I bring my lips to her belly, kissing it gently. She tenses at my touch but relaxes instantly. *Sensitive.* Got it.

"Did your doctor say it was okay for you to come here for a whole month this close to your due date?" She nods.

"What about work?" I pause in confusion. My stomach knots. "What about your mom?"

I avoid looking at her eyes, afraid at what I might find. Going no contact with my parents was the choice I wanted to make—the one I needed to make— but Hailey's relationship with her parents is nothing like mine. If she left them because she thinks this is what I need, I wouldn't be able to forgive myself.

"Eyes here," she says. "My siblings are stepping up to help with my mom, and she's stable. She has therapy and stuff, but she can be away from me for a while." She smiles reassuringly.

"I took the PTO I've been accruing for years. I guess when you feel guilty about taking time off, you don't realize how much you actually work until you go to use your PTO and the head nurse is surprised." She flashes me an alluring smile. "It was time for me to do something for me for once." She yawns again. She's trying to mask her exhaustion, but I know better.

I can't stop touching her bump. It's smooth and perfectly round. She must be exhausted, though, and as much as I don't want to let her go, she needs to relax.

"Let me run you a bath and you can relax. I have some friends coming over later, but I can cancel." I'm not letting her or our baby out of my sight, but she shakes her head.

"You have friends, Asher Hunter?" she sasses, completely derailing my thoughts.

I let out a harsh breath. "Very funny. Come on. Bath. Rest. Now."

I help her up and guide her to the bathroom, where I massage her back as the tub fills. Not too hot, not too cold. Perfect temperature for my perfect girl.

She's so stunning. Even with small bags under her eyes, she's glowing while growing the life inside her. The urge to keep her captive and take care of them invades all my senses. The bathroom light showcases every inch of her, and I want to touch and kiss and explore her body the way it looks now. I want to see all the things that have changed while she's been growing our baby, all the things that have stayed the same. I want to know this body as I know mine.

I trace her back with my hand, brushing her hair away just like I did that first night we met. I pepper kisses all the way up to her neck, my hands rounding her bump as my breathing speeds up. Damn, I love her always, but like this? Wow. It's like my brain forgot words and my world has no meaning beyond her, him, and us.

She shivers and squeezes my thigh. "Mmm. No. We're not doing anything. I need you to relax; you just traveled for so many hours." I kiss her neck again. "I'm taking care of you."

She moans when I massage her shoulders. "But you can jump in the water with me and make me feel good, no?"

"Behave," I grunt.

"I thought you were a water boy." Her breathy sounds bounce off the walls in the small bathroom.

"Prove it to me," she whispers, dragging her hands down her breasts, and over her belly.

Goddammit, I'm supposed to be doing the noble thing here, but I guess giving her an orgasm while she soaks in the water is technically taking care of her. I strip and carefully sit us both into the tub. I slide her in as she rests against me. I massage her shoulders, and she groans, my dick moving to attention.

"Someone's happy to see me," she whispers, sinking deeper, bringing her delicate hands to squeeze my thighs. "I love these."

"My legs?" I continue massaging, squeezing, touching, kissing, just like I wish I did for the past seven months I haven't been near her.

She lets out a sound between a groan and a moan. "Your thighs." I smile against her hair and continue massaging down her arms. My fingers find her hips, and when I dig in my fingertips, the pleasure it gives her is palpable. It's audible too.

Soft moans and whispered yeses.

Groans and moans.

A pleading.

A want.

And I'm about to give it all to her.

My fingers graze the top of her thigh, crawling slowly to the spot I know she wants me to touch. And if there was any doubt, when she drops her knees to open wider for me, she erases it.

"I like how it smells here," she mutters.

I've been trying to find her scent for years. The bottle in her house had no label, which led me to think she might buy it in bulk, but still, I can't find exactly what it is. "I'm trying to find what soap you use without asking you about it."

"You're never going to find it." My thumb presses over her clit, making her moan.

"I'm determined to find it," I mention, biting her earlobe. My desire for this woman has kept me alive more times than I can count, but touching her, smelling her, making her feel good, awakens something deep in me, something I can't recreate, just like the way she smells.

"I'll make you some."

I slide a finger inside her, and damn, she's tighter than I remember. So warm, tight, and perfect.

"You make your own soap?"

"Yes," she moans. "Remember the side business? Citrus & Oak? That's what I do. But please, stop talking about soap and make me come."

I lick her neck, holding one perfect breast while I tease her clit with the other one.

"Yes, ma'am."

I rub her nipple between my thumb and index finger until it's peaked to perfection. Her body has always been responsive to me or I've gotten to know everything that makes her tick. Either way, it ignites my soul. I've never felt more alive than when my fingers are buried inside her and all she can make are whispered sounds of pleasure. She squeezes my thigh with every slide of my finger.

She's so tight, so ready, and I just want her to let herself fall. Let herself feel good. I lower my hand from her breast, over her bump, and whisper in her ear, "You are always sexy, Hales. But you carrying our baby takes the number one spot for sexiest woman on Earth."

"Ash," she whispers, dropping her head back. The sweet, eldest daughter, always taking care of everyone; all she wants to hear is how good and perfect she is. I'll tell her until the day I die.

I slide another finger in. "You take my fingers so well." She arches her back. "You're my dream girl materialized."

"I think I'm going—"

I tsk. "I know you are." I press harder against her clit and squeeze her ass with my other hand. "Come for me, baby."

She rolls her ass and closes her legs, bucking against my hand. "Fuck," she whispers, and all I can do is thank whoever decided to send some good karma my way.

"SO THIS IS THE MYSTERY GIRL?" Silas asks.

"My girl. No mystery about it." I toss a napkin at him. My friends eventually arrived, and we've been together ever since. I don't celebrate the Fourth of July, but I'll take a day off when I can.

Silas is the newest of the crew, but he fits in perfectly. Travis retired last year, and Holt has been working training at A School since he was stationed in California. He's a great instructor, and they're lucky to have him. From the original crew, there are only a couple of us here, but it doesn't matter. We're all a family. We all carry our motto, *so others may live*, deep within us, no matter where we are.

"Hailey. You can just call me Hailey," she replies.

"How long are you staying for?" I knew the questions were going to come, but I was expecting them to come tomorrow, when I'm back at work.

"Not sure yet." Hailey yawns, sinking deeper into the chair.

"Alright, all of you have to go. My girl is sleepy."

"No, no. I can just go to sleep. It's been a long day."

I pretend to consider her, though I know deep down, there's nothing to consider. I don't want her to go to sleep without me, and I don't want to spend another second away from her if I don't have to. "They're leaving."

My friends take the hint, and between *nice to meet you* and *see you soon*, they leave us alone. I help her up and send her to our room while I get her a glass of water. *Our room.* I could get used to this.

"You know I could've gotten the water myself, right?" she says, taking a sip and setting the glass on her night stand next to her CPAP. I'm so glad she finally listened to me when I told her she gasped in her sleep a couple times on our dates—the dates where she didn't hang up the phone and I ended up watching her sleep for hours. It was the best sight and the most comforting sound until I realized that wasn't normal. My girl has sleep apnea and has to wear the machine. She's so cute wearing it too. Even if she hates it, I think it's great. It's keeping her alive, so I'll take it.

"I'm about to pamper you so hard, you won't know what to do with yourself." I step behind her, wrapping my arms around her waist and resting my hands on her perfect round bump.

"Let someone take care of *you* for once," I whisper, resting my face on her shoulder. "Let *me*." She nods and lies in bed, patting the spot next to her for me to jump in. Which I do, pulling her back to me. Her ass nestled against me, my hand around her belly, I realize I want to touch this bump every second of the time I'll have her here with me. This, her growing our baby, is the closest thing to magic I've ever experienced, and I somehow feel like if I don't touch her, if I don't feel it, it will disappear.

I want this—her here, them here—more than I want anything else. Would I be good at this? I have zero experience with decent parents. Is there a genetic marker for it? Am I doomed before I even start? I love this baby and this woman so much; I just want to do right by them. I caress her belly, and she relaxes against me more.

Give me a sign, little one.

Almost as if I conjured it into existence, our baby kicks. Hard.

I tense, but Hailey softly giggles. "He's usually not this active at night, so he likes you."

He kicks again, and my heart heals a little more. Hailey being here, in my arms, with our baby moving for me to feel him, I know my heart never knew love until this.

Until her.

I will do everything in my power to make sure she knows that, to make sure she knows how much I love her and what I'm willing to do for them. For our little growing family.

"I like him too," I whisper, my face buried in her hair. It's right here I know I've found peace. And for once, I close my eyes without fear as I fall asleep.

9

SEPTEMBER 2031

Yellow by Kina Grannis

ASHER

"DO you want me to take him?" Damien, Hailey's brother, asks, and I shake my head. He hands me a beer, the bottle cooling my hands, and sits across from me.

"You've been holding him for hours. If my mom sees, she'll say you'll spoil him." We clink our bottles and stay in comfortable silence. I've been here for a week now, but I need to go back soon. In two days, to be exact. I don't know how I'm supposed to go back to the cold and leave the warmth that is being with her family.

Hailey is like the glue of her family. I've deduced that fact through the years getting to know her, but nothing could've prepared me to see it in action. Everyone sticks to her like the sausage gravy her dad made that went cold. They're one big unit with plenty of things that make them unique, but like vines, their lives intertwine.

It's beautiful to watch and incredibly heart wrenching. It's unfortunate so many children grow up with no clue that love like this can exist. It's unfortunate I didn't know these types of families existed beyond movies.

Until now.

I'm so glad she didn't stay in Alaska. I'm so glad she knew her heart and body needed to be here, near her family. I've missed her so much, I would've been selfish and ask her to stay if I didn't know this is what's best for her. *For them.*

"Love doesn't spoil a child." My reply is sharp; I'm so overwhelmed with emotion, I don't know what else to do. In two days, I have to say goodbye to Cash, this sweet baby who keeps waking us up every ten minutes.

Goodbye to quiet breakfasts with him latched to his mom's breast.

Goodbye to laughter and warm meals brought by Hailey's siblings or parents, dad jokes from her father while we were in the hospital for the never-ending labor. I have to ask her why she never told me she had a built-in dad joke factory right at her house when I was trying so hard to make her smile with mine.

"I know we don't know each other well, but are you okay?" Damian wipes the sweat off his forehead, and I smile bittersweetly.

The soft groan from the little bundle of joy getting restless in my arms suddenly makes everything clear. I know what I need to do. The thought settles as I watch a cardinal flying through the bright green grass, landing quietly on the paved porch.

I nod. "Yeah, I'm just in love."

His laughter could go a mile as his smile reaches his eyes. "We are all well aware how in love with Hailey you are."

I'm glad they can tell, because I don't want them to have any doubts how I feel about their sister.

How do I tell him I'm in love with this whole thing, though? With the way this family operates, the way this baby is filling holes in my heart I didn't know existed. With the idea of having a family like this one day, so full of love, companionship, and laughter. I want this.

"I'm glad." They're the only words I'm able to say when Cash's broken cry breaks free. "That's my cue." Damien nods, and I rest the untouched beer on the table and head to find this kid's nipples.

I knock on the door, careful not to startle him and clutching him close to my chest. *I've got you buddy. Always.*

"Come in!" Hailey announces. "There he is. I was wondering where you'd taken him."

A week postpartum, and I'm in awe of this woman, especially as she effortlessly takes Cash from my arms and latches him on.

She's breathtaking.

She walks to the rocking chair that once belonged to her mother. Each sister used it, and now, it's her turn.

This is what every baby should have. Parents, grandparents, uncles and aunts, all who grew up in loved homes.

In homes where children, *their children*, are wanted, loved, and cherished, not just tolerated.

What a joy it is to witness it first hand, and it puts me even more at peace with my decision to go no contact with my parents.

Cash will never know the feeling that became my normal all my life, and I'm fine with that. I rather be a great dad and husband, not a son who searches validation from people who don't deserve it.

I know what I have to do.

I know what I *want* to do.

The only sounds are Cash's little grunts as he feeds and my heart thumping loud in my chest. I get the undeniable urge to just tell her my plans, but I don't, not until I can figure out if I can pull it off. I need to find a way of living here, with them, surrounded by this joy— even if I have to find a different passion at work.

So many things can fulfill my career, but nothing compares to the feeling of belonging I have here.

"What?" Hailey asks looking up at me, a grin spreading across her face to match mine.

My fingers brush across her hair as I dip to kiss the top of her head. I linger longer than usual and take it all in.

Yup, no doubt in my mind.

This is where I belong. Maybe if I'm here, I can take some of the load off Hailey's shoulders.

Months ago, I knew they were my peace, but this is the reminder I needed.

They're my life.

10

NEW YEAR'S EVE 2031

New Years Day by Taylor Swift & Make You Feel My Love by Glee Cast

HAILEY

"SH, sh, sh, it's okay. Daddy's coming." I kiss the top of Cash's head and look at the clock.

Same time as last time.

Of course, Hailey. You just looked at it ten seconds ago.

He said he would be here and that he had a surprise for me. I don't care about surprises; I just want to see him. Long distance relationships are one thing, but raising a baby while missing the love of my life is for the birds.

I miss him and I want him.

I glance at the open door and tuck hair behind my ear, not dragging my lip to my mouth like I would've before. It's incredible how much you start healing when you quit a soul sucking job, even if, once upon a time, it filled your soul.

No more lip biting, nail scratching, random ass pacing in the middle of the day.

Quitting and therapy.

Boundaries and replaced behaviors.

I've never felt better—until now.

Until my eyes light up meeting his brown ones, framed by sexy glasses, full of life and never leaving mine. Until his smile reaches the corner of his eyes, and little lines of a life well lived come to the surface. Because with Asher standing at my door with two giant bags, his mustache, beard, and hair sprinkled with grays that make him look even better, I'm so happy, I don't even know what to do with myself.

"Hales," he whispers with such joy behind his words, it reaches my toes. I forget words and rhyme and reason. I forget time. I forget it all.

"See, I told you Daddy was coming." I close the space between us, giving him a quick peck on his lips. "Hi."

He smiles wider, pulling us tight to his body. "Let me bring the bags in and wash my hands so I can pick him up, yeah?"

I follow him inside, waiting for him to do just that, while I bounce Cash in my arms.

"Come here, little one. I've missed you."

He takes Cash, brushing his fingers over my skin and leaving the trace of cardamom behind. I've known Asher for six years now, and I'm still not over the fact that he smells like coffee on an early morning or spicy tea before reading your favorite book. Maybe it was his scent that made me fall in love this hard for him, or maybe the way he talks to me, or how he doesn't trust his heart to anyone, but he trusted it to me.

And definitely the glasses. They do it for me, every time.

He sits in the corner of the living room and pats the spot next to him. Another New Year's Eve next to him, maybe the last one we'll be apart. I transitioned out of the hospital and have been working selling soaps, lotions, and candles locally. I can do that from Alaska, right? At least, that's what I tell myself.

I can't do this long distance thing anymore, even if I'll miss everyone here with all my heart. I guess I'm destined to miss someone at all times—him if I'm here, and them if I'm there—but I refuse to ask him to give up his true love, rescuing, just to move here with me.

"I have a question for you," Asher says, not lifting his gaze from his son.

I sit across from him and cross my legs, waiting for whatever it is he wants to tell me. "I might have an answer."

"You know how every year on my birthday, you've never asked me about what I want as a gift, but you always have something for me?"

Well, that's because in the second year we were together, he told me he has never gotten a gift just for him or that he never asked for. He said he had never been surprised by anything, and how sad is that? So, every year, I've made it my mission to give him something that reminds me of him, even if small, but a surprise, nonetheless.

I nod, brushing my bangs off my face. "I'm sorry. I thought you liked those."

His smile widens. "What have we said about apologizing?" I roll my eyes in exasperation. "Stop being a brat and tell me."

"We don't apologize for existing." I swear, he and my therapist are conspiring against me. Or in favor of me, I guess.

His gaze flickers between our son and me. "I love that you do that. It makes me feel special because you took time out of your busy day to get something for me, but this year, I want to ask for something specific."

My fingers gently trace the seam of the chair. "It might be hard to find on short notice, but I can definitely try. What is it?"

"I want to be your husband."

The words rattle me like windows in a storm. "What?"

His laughter breaks through the emotional rollercoaster in my brain. "Look who's sticking to the monosyllabic words now."

I laugh at that. It's incredible how his words and his presence can make me feel at ease, and judging by how calm Cash is, I think he feels it too. Asher is so good for our nervous systems. But wait—back to the question at hand.

"You said you wanted something specific for your birthday."

He nods.

"But then you said—"

"That I want to be your husband." He interrupts.

My breath catches in my throat. "You can't just come in here and tell me you want to be my husband."

He shrugs. "I mean I could ask you to be my wife if you'd prefer, but I really want you to know how much I'm already yours, how much I crave to be your husband. It's beyond a want. It's a need."

He smiles, and I sink.

I melt. I disappear.

"If you want me back, I would love to make that happen." He winks. "It can be the best birthday gift anyone has ever given me . . . which is pretty big, considering you've given me some really good ones."

"I don't know what to say," I mutter.

He's so calm. So quiet. So still. So unnervingly at peace.

"You could say, "Yes, Asher, I would love for you to be my husband" or "no, I don't want to." Clearly, only one is the right answer, but if your answer is the second one . . . I'll just have to try to convince you this whole lifetime."

He kisses Cash's forehead. "And the next."

Asher stands, placing our baby boy in the bassinet next to the worn couch I've had since I was in college. He walks toward me and looks down so his chestnut eyes meet mine.

"I was just kidding, by the way." He pulls a ring from his pocket and gets on one knee, his smile radiating so much joy.

"Of course I was going to ask. Hailey Fox, you already make me the happiest man in the world. You have shown me so much about life, love, and myself with your selflessness—and selfishly, I just want you all to myself. Forever." He smiles, and a tear breaks free from his eye, tracing his cheek and landing in his mustache. "I would be so honored to call you my wife."

I throw myself at him, hugging tightly around his neck.

"Is that a yes, Hales?"

I hold him tighter. "That's a hell yes." I put some distance between us so he can see the happiness in my eyes, beyond what I can convey with my words.

I want him to see the tears of joy trickling down my face, how much I'm shaking.

I want him to see my love for him in every gold speckle in my eyes.

I want him to know how there is no doubt in my mind it's his arms I'm meant to be in.

He slides the beautiful ring on, and then it hits me. "So I'm moving to Alaska?"

He shakes his head, surprising me. "Oh, I didn't tell you? I'm not going back."

"What?"

Our joint laughter bounces in the space, startling Cash and making me smile.

"I got him." Asher drops my hand, shaking his head, and speed-walks to our son as I admire the pretty pink diamond on my finger.

He holds our boy in his arms, sliding a paci into his mouth and coming back to me. He's bouncing, calming him as if it's the most natural thing in the world, as if being a dad is the easiest thing for him.

"I have a job here, in Baker." He kisses the baby's forehead before holding my hand in his. "Working for Florida Rescue."

"But being a rescue swimmer was your dream."

He shakes his head, his eyes full of glee. "You were my dream all along. I just needed to find you. I'm ready to be the present father and partner I've always wanted to be. I'm ready to take care of you."

"I don't need you to."

"I want to. For once in my life, I'm happy."

He looks at our son, smiling softly before continuing. "For once in my life, I feel like I know my purpose."

Cash stirs in his arms, and I grab him—it's boob time. I latch him quickly, looking back at Asher, who starts to lead me back to the couch. "You two are my purpose, and I can't wait for our new life together."

He sits next to me, placing his feet on the table and draping mine over his legs. With his arm around me and our son safe on my chest, I know this is exactly where I belong too. "Thank you."

"For what?" he asks against my hair.

"For loving me even when I'm not perfect."

I can feel his smile against my head. "Oh, baby, you're pretty perfect to me. I should be the one thanking you for showing me what love truly is. Thank you for showing me this was the reason."

I wait for him to continue.

"I waited all my life for this season, and even though it has been long awaited, it was definitely worth it." He smiles, and I suddenly forget everything but him. "And I'd do it again if this is the outcome."

11

EPILOGUE: NEW YEARS EVE 2035

All My Life by K-Ci and JoJo

ASHER

"HAPPY BIRTHDAY, dear Daddy, Happy birthday to you!" Cash and Hailey sing while she bounces Hollie on her hip.

I blow out the candles on the double chocolate cake we baked earlier today, as is tradition for us now, but I have no need to make a wish. Everything I could ever want was granted to me ten years ago when I accidentally spilled that drink on Hailey's dress.

I give Cash a kiss on the top of his head and grab Hollie from Hailey's hands.

"You didn't close your eyes," Hailey whispers against my ear while passing me the baby. "Your wish won't come true."

I smile at our sleepy baby before looking at my beautiful wife. "I told you last year and the year before, and the year before that . . . " I kiss Hollie's forehead, and she cuddles against my chest, closing her pretty grey eyes that match her mama's.

"My unspoken wishes have come true, and all I want is for a life-time with all of you."

Hailey rolls her eyes, as sassy as ever. "Keep your voice low then. She's about to go to sleep. I can't believe she's still up."

I don't have to look at the clock to know it's midnight. Just like she promised, Hailey has been keeping the kids up to wish me a happy birthday right as the clock strikes midnight every year. She wants me to know how much she loves spending another year with me and that she won't ever let me forget.

Like I could.

"Come on, Cash. Let's go night night," she says, offering him her pinky and walking away as I wave our son goodnight.

I stay in the living room, swaying to K-Ci and JoJo playing in the background as fireworks explode in the distance. We wanted another baby, and even though it took a couple years, Hollie finally came, and she's absolutely perfect. If it was up to me, Hailey would always be pregnant. She disagrees with me, though, and since it's her body, she gets the final call.

Hollie's heavy breathing interrupts my thoughts, and after laying her down in her pink crib in her dark, starry sky bedroom, I walk back out to the living room, where Hailey waits for me. Her hair is up in a top bun, her pretty bangs styled the familiar way I love, a glass of wine in hand. I join her, propping her legs on top of my lap as soon as I sit across from her on the soft couch.

She takes a sip of the dark liquid, sliding her tongue over the rim of the glass, and my dick stands in attention immediately. One simple move, and I want her. I always want her.

It seems like if our bodies are not intertwined, I can't breathe prop-erly, can't think straight.

The one place where I know I belong is with her—inside her heart, by her side, and between her legs.

"So, thirty one, huh?" I shrug at her question, and she continues in amusement, "Such an old man."

I smirk, testing the water and seeing if she's in the same mindset. When she returns my smile, I know she is. "I heard the thirties are the new twenties."

"Actually better." Hailey sinks deeper into the couch, her eyes closing as a smile paints her face. Gosh—breathtaking. "Do you miss it?"

The question takes me by surprise. "Miss what?"

I know exactly what she means, but I want to make sure I answer correctly. I'm a maritime instructor now—you can't keep me out of the water for long—and it's been years since my last rescue mission. I'm happy though. Can't she see that?

The storm behind her cloudy eyes tells a story I wasn't expecting to hear today. Does she really think I regret anything in my life? She sighs. "Your job."

"I have a job."

"You know what I mean. Ocean cowboying, rescuing people, the whole thing." There's true worry in her face, the same I saw in her the day I decided next to her was my place. Hailey has always been a woman of words. Showing her with actions has never been enough, and I'm not sure why I thought now would be a good time.

We vowed to always communicate, to tell each other everything, but somewhere along the way, I forgot to tell her she's my purpose. My happiness. My all.

I sit forward, holding her hands, willing her to look at me. "I told you once in a letter why I wanted to do that job, right?"

She nods but stays quiet, letting me continue. "For a long time, the only thing I could hope for, wish for, even pray for was a job where I felt like I was helping. I didn't even think there was a possibility of anything else for me."

My eyes travel over her, making sure she not only hears me, but she feels every single one of my words as I continue, "I couldn't even dream of being loved the way you love me. I couldn't even dream of finding what you and I have, because Hales, I never knew it existed."

She smiles, but it doesn't reach her eyes—not because she's sad, though. No, it's something else I can't quite name.

"I don't know how to express that our life is beyond my wildest dreams. I wouldn't trade you, Cash, or Hollie for the world. Ever." I tilt my head to the side, and she mimics my movements.

"I thought my purpose in life was to rescue others, to help in the most daunting circumstances, but I realized every single day that led me to the decision to enlist was with one purpose and one purpose only."

The words dance in the air like the instrumental music in movie scenes—powerful for whatever the moment is meant to convey.

Can she hear the silence between each word?

Can she understand the meaning?

Do my words translate what my heart is feeling?

"To meet you."

She gasps.

"Don't act surprised now. You know it was always you."

"Yeah, and it was always you too, but that doesn't mean I'm your whole life's purpose, babe." She's so serious, as if what she's hearing is completely delusional and irrational. As if it's not true.

I pull her to me, her ass landing on my lap and her hands shifting up to hold my face.

I look at her.

No, I stare.

I stare until she shivers. I stare until there's no doubt in her mind I mean it wholeheartedly.

"You are. You were, even before we met. Our souls were so connected, I didn't feel alive until lightning crashed into my eyes that night ten years ago."

I kiss her forehead, because if I kiss her lips, I won't be able to finish the sentiment. I need to touch her. To kiss her. To have her.

"You asked me why I was so quiet that night, and the truth is, I couldn't find words. Somehow, my whole body knew we were meant to be more."

My gaze drops to her lips and quickly flits back to her eyes. "My life not only gained purpose, but my soul and my heart did too. My body belongs to you. My heart belongs to you."

I kiss her lips this time—not deep, not passionate, just a flash reminder that my lips are hers too. "Everything I have is yours. I don't need anything else but the three of you."

"That's not healthy."

I shrug. "Didn't you say once that I was insane for expecting different outcomes while doing the same thing?"

She nods, narrowing her eyes, knowing exactly which direction this is going. "I'm not well. I'm hopelessly and irrevocably in love with you, and truly, nothing much matters. Jobs will come and go, but you and I will remain."

"Asher," she whispers, her words so soft, they could dance on their tiptoes.

"Until we're old and gray." And then, she kisses me. She shows me how much she knows damn well I mean it and how much she loves me back.

She smiles against my lips. "The stars aligned, huh?"

"They did. Just for you and me."

NOT READY TO SAY GOODBYE? Read Asher's POV at the wedding and the moment he realized how he felt about Hailey in the bonus epilogue here! Or go to https://www.acordovabooks.com/playlists

CURIOUS ABOUT LIVIE, Hailey's best friend? Read her story here! It's a Rom Com!

ACKNOWLEDGMENTS

What a journey this book was! If you're reading this, it means you gave my super bizarre idea a chance, and I cannot tell you how grateful I am for it. Hailey and Asher are some of my favorite characters I've ever written, and I'm so glad I got to share them with you.

I have so many people to say thank you to, but I want to start with YOU, because without your love for my stories and your support, I wouldn't be here. This story would probably not exist if it wasn't for you, so thank you.

Thank you to my favorite and best surprise ever, Joey. There's always some of you in all my main characters, and that's no different for this one. What a funny thing that you decided to go to that one party all those years ago, even though you didn't want to, and met me. You changed my life with one look, one touch, and one whispered hello.

To my alphas and betas, Maeghen, Mandy, Adriana, Colleen, and Sierra, thank you for jumping into reading my work even when it's last minute. This story was so different, and you loving them makes me incredibly emotional.

To my bestie author girls Hollie Luckie and Sarah A. Bailey for always saying 'you can do it' when I'm completely delusional about timelines.

To my kids, because you two were the most perfect surprise. Forever and always mine.

To my editing team, Jayné and Alexa, thank you for always saying yes! Even when I'm like "Hi, surprise, I wrote something else."

To Mayhara from Mayharate for the most beautiful illustration and to Kim from KBG cover design for not yelling at me when I needed this done so quickly.

To Cassie, my brand manager and PA . . . I don't even know what to say, because thank you isn't enough. I don't know what I would do without you and Cassie's Creative. Thank you. Thank you. Thank you.

To my Patreon babes! Your support means the absolute world to me. Especially to Scarther and Nancy—thank you for supporting my dream in this HUGE way.

And last but not least, thank you to Joey again. Thank you for being everything I needed and more, for taking care of me even when I don't know I need it.

Now off to cry in author tears and onto the next book.

143,
Ambar

ABOUT THE AUTHOR

GRAB A BOOK, FALL IN LOVE, STAY A WHILE ♥

Ambar writes heartfelt, diverse, and emotional romance. Her stories are multicultural with a focus on raw storytelling and flawed characters who drive the plot forward with their challenges and growth. She has independently published four complete novels and two novellas, all featuring interracial couples with a range of dynamics. Her books are open-door romances that evoke tears, with high tension and delicious happily ever afters.

When Ambar is not writing she's chasing chickens or children, going on adventures with her family, crying over fictional people, dancing and reading in her she shed. Ambar enjoys boat rides, traveling, and spending time outside.